DESPERATE MEASURES

THE BREAKING THROUGH SERIES BOOK 2

BARBARA DELEO

FOREWORD

This title was previously published, in part, as Last Chance Proposal.

1

____

As the sun of a New Zealand summer's day burnt through his black T-shirt, Cy Hathaway bent and peered in the old hall window. He scrubbed the heel of his hand across a fine film of dust and cobwebs, screwed one eye shut, and peered in.

Rows of people in shorts and T-shirts sat facing the front, listening intently to the presentation. His heart drummed deep in his chest, jet lag and the anticipation of what he was about to do scrambling his thoughts. It wasn't the meeting that had drawn him to this hall from the other side of the world. It was the speaker, Ellie Jacobs. A girl from his past, someone he hadn't seen in eight years. And if everything went according to his carefully constructed plan, the woman who'd soon be his stand-in wife.

Despite this being the longest shot known to humankind—and the most selfish thing he'd ever asked—he couldn't leave New Zealand until she agreed to marry him. He'd managed to get the grandparents to give him two weeks with his son over Christmas, but after that . . .

Ellie Jacobs was his last chance.

If only she could forgive him for everything he'd done.

He pushed open the heavy door and a crowd of bodies twisted as one on their regulation wooden benches. The hall hadn't changed since he'd left as a teenager. Dust motes shimmied in the air, and the place still smelled of hot sun on polished wood. Red and green Christmas decorations trailed haphazardly from the ceiling, and the portrait of a young Queen Elizabeth hung crooked on the wall.

"I'll be staying at Starfish Cottage, if anyone has more questions in the next few..." The lyrical voice from the front faded to nothing.

"Hi." He lifted a hand and his words echoed in the quiet corners of the hall. "Sorry I'm late. Holiday traffic, and I forgot what these country roads can be like. Hoped I'd get here earlier."

There were murmured hellos and the man next to him stood, his blue eyes twinkling under bushy brows. "Cy, great to see you. It's been a long time, son."

He smiled and took Jack Parker's extended hand, but his gaze was glued to the lectern. Was that Ellie? That stunning woman in black trousers and a white blouse, fingers pressed to her lips and eyes rounded in surprise? He'd thought about her constantly since the notice of the meeting arrived like a talisman at his home in Colorado. When he'd read her explanation of the restoration she was heading in Rata Cove, and seen her flowing signature at the bottom of the glossy announcement, he'd remembered her big heart, genuine smile, and generous spirit, and knew she was the answer. But it was the face of the eighteen-year-old girl he'd known that filled his mind then, not this confident, poised woman. The long blonde hair she'd worn wild and free as a teenager was now pulled away in a high ponytail, her blue eyes wide. "Cy, it's good to see you."

Memories of summers spent with her flooded him as he settled on the hard wooden bench. The scent of Coppertone sunscreen. The endless ball games on scorching sand, snorkeling in the warm, clear water of the cove. One day stuck hard in his mind. The one and only time he and Ellie had made love. That day, and the life-changing consequences of their actions, seared into his memory.

Realizing Ellie and everyone in the hall was now staring at him, he pulled his thoughts to the present. "I hear some changes are happening here."

"Yes." Ellie cleared her throat before tapping notes on the lectern. Tortoiseshell reading glasses sat on her nose and made her look as confident and in control as she sounded. And she rocked the sexy librarian look that was doing strange things to his chest. "You've read the information I sent about the restoration project?" She smiled, and the warmth on her face was a tonic to his jet-lagged brain.

"I'd love to hear more."

"As you've read, the council's employed me to lead a restoration project on some of the buildings near the beach. The hall, the old library, the boardwalk in particular, and some of the holiday homes." She pushed a lock of hair from her face. "I'm looking for community input before I finalize my plans." She paused and hooked him with her gaze. "I don't recall seeing you at any of the initial meetings." She glanced down at her notes, then slowly back up at him, and his chest constricted for the time he'd lost with her and the strangers they'd become. "I don't have a submission from you, do I?"

"No, I. . . ah . . . I thought I'd be more help by being here." He hadn't been to Rata Cove, this tiny coastal New Zealand town in nearly a decade, didn't have a right to be part of this, and he wouldn't have returned if he didn't have to ask the biggest favor of his life. "So, where do things stand?"

Ellie glanced at her watch. "This meeting's run its course, Cy. We've been discussing my restoration plans for close to an hour and we need to move out for the New Year's pageant practice."

"I've just arrived in the cove." Weariness filtered into his voice as he dug a hand through his hair. "But I'll take you up on the offer to answer my questions at your cottage."

Ellie nodded, then after a little more general discussion, closed the meeting and people ambled from the hall into the brilliant sunshine. He moved against the flow to reach her, greeting people he hadn't seen in years. One of his old surfing mates said hi and introduced Cy to his kids, and Tom from the store slapped him on the back and told him to stop by for a chat and the town's famous meat pie. As he drew closer to the front, he caught the end of conversations.

"We're so lucky to have you do this, Ellison," an elderly man said as he tipped his cap to her. "Things have been looking tired and run-down for years. We've all got faith you'll turn things around and people will holiday in the cove again."

"Thanks so much, Max." She touched the old guy's wrinkled hand. "It's great to have everyone's support."

"Thank you, Ellie. Harry and I can't wait to see the changes you're going to make," Betty Browning said as she shooed small children in front of her. "It seems like yesterday you were performing in the New Year's pageant on this stage, and now look at you. All grown up and important and living in different countries around the world."

Ellie's eyes sparkled as she smiled.

When the last of the people had moved away, Cy stepped forward and the air between them stilled.

"Ellie, it's great to see you."

Her back straightened, and she clasped her hands in front. Of course she wouldn't lean in for a kiss on the cheek. He hadn't spoken to her since the day after she'd said she loved him, and he'd turned his back on her and left the cove for good. And he couldn't blame her one bit.

Her lips rolled together, and her penetrating gaze hooked his. "To be honest, I was a bit stunned when you walked through the door. I thought you lived in the States. That's where I sent the homeowner's meeting notice. No one's been at your holiday house for ages."

Lines of tension played around her eyes. Her questioning gaze drifted across his face. In eight years, she'd become even more radiant, more animated than he remembered. The beauty of a girl had bloomed into a gorgeous woman, but frost hung in her tone.

"It's been a long time." The words of a detached stranger had come out his mouth before he could stop them. He'd never been unsettled talking to beautiful women before, but this was Ellie, someone who, despite his best intentions, he'd hurt badly. "So, you're an architect, right? Specializing in coastal properties?"

"Yes." A smile played at her lips as she picked up her suit jacket from the back of a chair and put it on. She shook her head and a soft blonde ringlet escaped from her ponytail. "I just can't believe you're here. I've caught up with your mum and sister over the years, and they've missed seeing you back in the cove for holidays."

She'd changed so much and yet hardly at all. But there was something new, a secret, womanly power he could sense growing the longer he stood there. Of course, he'd thought about her through the years, regretting they'd lost touch, wishing he'd done more to build a bridge after all they'd been through. Looking at her now, though, no one would know the dark places she'd come from. Seeing this confidence in her confirmed she was the perfect choice for his custody plan, and if that all went well, who knew how their relationship might develop?

He slung hands in the pockets of his chinos. "I can't believe I waited so long to come back. Knowing how much you've always loved the cove, I understand how important this restoration must be for you, Ellie. I'd like to know more."

She picked up the small leather satchel and held it in front of her. "I'm really sorry, but I don't have time to talk now. My sister Fleur and her son Louis are here for Christmas, but let's catch up sometime."

Catch up sometime? He shouldn't have expected her to be more welcoming, but it was a slug to the heart. He rocked back on his heels. "Fleur and Louis? Wow, he was just a baby when I last saw him."

She nodded and glanced toward the door.

"No problem, we can catch up later," he said. "Do you live here now?"

She laughed. "I wish. Work takes me around the country and the world, but I try to get back to the cove for the holidays. I'll be spending the next few months managing the start of this restoration, then I'm off to an island in Greece for the rest of the year." She grinned and lifted an eyebrow. "It's a tough job but someone's gotta do it." She flicked her wrist and looked at a bright blue watch. "Sorry, but I need to open the cottage for Fleur. You can ask questions about the project while walking there if you like."

He nodded and followed her out into the sunshine.

∾

When Ellie pushed her way out into the December after-noon, Cy fell into step beside her. His warm citrus scent kicked up her heartbeat.

"Want me to carry that?" He nodded at her briefcase. "It looks impressively heavy."

She still couldn't believe he was here. The shock of seeing him again lay like a piece of cold stone in her gut. Not that he'd ever know. "I'm fine, thanks."

He looked so different. What had once been a mess of curls kissed golden by hours in the surf, was now the salon cut of a city dweller, glossy and neat. Where multicolored board shorts would've hung low on slim hips, tan chinos contrasted with a black T-shirt.

For so many years she'd imagined this moment, seeing his dazzling smile again, the confident way he walked into a room, but in her dreams it was never like this. Never with him standing like a stranger, asking her about a business project, and she couldn't think of one intelligent thing to say.

She hadn't counted on him being part of the project closest to her heart, though, and she'd have to deal with it. The longer she spent in Cy Hathaway's company, the quicker she'd fall under his spell—it had happened a hundred times before—but not this time. When she'd told him she loved him all those years ago, he'd turned tail and run, and she'd never put herself in that vulnerable, devas-tated position again.

"How long are you back?" She kept her attention forward, following the shade from the red-and-green *pōhutukawa* trees nodding over the sand. Cicadas played a symphony in the background, and seagulls hovered in an endless blue sky.

"A couple weeks. There's…" He cleared his throat. "I

need to deal with some things." As he turned to her, his tone shifted. "I think what you're doing here is amazing."

Slowing her steps, she squeezed the handle of her satchel. "Thanks. It's great that the council agreed to fund the restoration. I was really pleased to be asked to oversee it. There's not a lot of time and spare cash for the upkeep of towns like this. I approached the council last year and offered my services and they agreed to let me renovate."

He turned and stared hard at her, his blue eyes shining and her heart did a loop. "You mean, you're doing this for nothing? That must be tough."

She lifted a shoulder and looked him in the eye. "I love this place. It has memories that would've been lost if something wasn't done. It was a no-brainer. My project in Greece should help pay the bills. As long as I get this finished in time."

"They're lucky to have you. My sister tells me you're an expert in your field."

A fizz shot up her spine, and she stepped back. He'd been talking to his sister about her? "I love this place too much to let it die."

He scuffed a boot through talc-like sand. "As soon as your letter arrived, I knew I had to come back."

She'd never contacted him after he left, knew that what lay between them was too overpowering to be repaired. "I sent letters to all the homeowners, of course. Not just you."

He nodded, and she continued. "I was surprised you were listed as the owner. Did you buy your parents and sister out?"

He bunched hands deep in his pockets and the fabric of his shirt pulled tight across his broad, muscled shoulders. "Mum and Kelly don't come here anymore. After Dad finally left, they found the maintenance difficult."

She hid her surprise. His father had left his mother? Cy had been so hurt by his father's affairs, the drama of his parents' relationship when they were teenagers. "How often do you get back to New Zealand from the States?"

"Not much." He looked out to sea, and a muscle flexed at his jaw. That he was even more handsome than he'd been as a teenager seemed impossible, but it was true. His eyes seemed bluer. His cheekbones more pronounced, lips fuller. "I own a chain of surf stores across the U.S, so I travel a lot. One of my competitors has been looking to buy me out, but I've worked hard to build the business, and I enjoy the challenge of running stores in different states."

He hadn't been back in the few summers Ellie had been here recently. She knew because she'd lost count of the times she'd stood outside his house in a swimsuit and bare feet, daydreaming about what it would be like if they still spent warm days here together. With his family, her sister Fleur, and nephew Louis . . . and maybe a couple of kids of their own.

She shook her head to remove the crazy little fantasy that sprung itself on her when she least expected it. Years ago they'd made love one tangled, passionate time, and then he'd left and never returned. She was the girl whose grief he'd made his own. He was the boy who still shared a brutal secret. She flicked a piece of hair from her face. "So, if you're here for Christmas, I guess you'll have family coming. I haven't seen your mother or Kelly in years. I'd love to spend time with them."

He picked up a shell and threw it out to sea. "They won't be making it this year."

Something tugged inside her. Cy had come all this way and wouldn't be spending Christmas with his family? Something wasn't right.

Share it with us, she almost said. *Come and have an orphans' Christmas with Fleur and me and Louis while my parents riverboat down the Danube, or whichever way they'd planned to avoid Christmas at the cove for another year.* But the words jammed in her throat. Cy seemed preoccupied, closed even, and she wasn't sure how he'd respond.

His voice was hollow. "It'll just be the two of us for Christmas."

"The two of you?"

"Me and my son, Jonty."

"Your son." The beat of her heart almost hijacked her words. "How old is he?"

A dark shadow crawled across his features. She knew the answer. The grim set of his face gave it away.

"He's six."

Her blood turned to ice as the familiar vision of her brother's six-year-old, lifeless body being pulled from the surf stamped for the millionth time in her mind. Her heart thudded, small and cramped in her throat. She set up the barriers as she'd always done, but the pain broke through.

Breathe.

"Ellie, I—"

He turned to her and she swung her attention to the sand to avoid his tortured stare. The day that changed so many lives. They'd been kissing on a yacht when they should've been watching William. He'd know the chill dancing across her skin, the crater widening in her chest.

Her body quaked, and he stepped closer before seeming to think better of it and kept on talking. "My son's never been here. Katie Newport's looking after him at the moment." He shook his head as they drew up in front of his family's holiday home. Surrounded by bleached logs and waist-high seagrass, it seemed to snooze on the sand. "I can't believe she's sixteen."

"I know, it's scary, right? The way time passes."

"Jonty's finding everything strange." He scraped a hand across his jaw. "Being somewhere so new without his own things around him, it's tough."

"So he's never been to New Zealand at Christmas?"

"He's only been to Auckland once when he was two. But that wasn't with me. He's never been to the beach."

She couldn't help the surprise flitter across her face. "You own surf stores and he's never been to the beach?"

"We live in Colorado, that's—" He shifted his eyes away. "We *have* to live in Colorado."

The sun's rays through the trees freckled on his skin as he crossed his arms.

"Is that where his mother lives?"

An indefinable cloud cast across Cy's features, and she could've kicked herself for her question.

You hardly know him anymore. She swallowed. *If you ever did.* "I'm sorry." She waved her hand in apology. "I have no right asking."

"Do you have children?"

She squeezed the handle of the briefcase tighter. "No, I don't. My career's taking off and I'm doing projects all over the world. That's my passion. My love." Movement out the corner of her eye caused her to turn, and from Cy's house came Katie Newport and a small boy with tousled, corn-colored hair. The image of his dad.

"Bringing families back to this place is so important." He looked at his son. "I want Jonty to have the same holidays I did growing up here. The outdoors, the sense of community, the innocence." He threw her a heart-stopping smile, and her skin tingled. "I might live in the States, but I want to know what's going on here. Sorry I missed all the important information at the meeting. Could we meet up to talk later?"

She bit her lip as she watched Katie encouraging the little boy to come forward. Each time the girl tried to touch him, he wrenched his body away and stood staring at them, a brightly colored scarf wound like a bandage around his hand.

Cy walked toward him but stopped a few feet away and crouched, his voice holding a tenderness that misted her vision. "Hey, bud. I bet you had fun with Katie."

The boy didn't reply, but kept staring past his father to Ellie as Cy spoke quietly. "Why don't we go up to the house and have a snack, eh?"

Still, the boy stood rigid and silent.

"I have to get to New Year's pageant practice, Mr. Hathaway," Katie said.

"Sure, Katie. Thanks for looking after Jonty." He paused and tension wrapped around his words. "Was everything all right?"

The pretty girl smiled, but concern creased her flawless forehead. "He didn't want to do anything other than sit on the bed with his scarf. I tried to get him to build a sandcastle but he wouldn't."

"Don't worry. I shouldn't have left him." His voice was light, but the depth of concern on Cy's face hit Ellie like a blunt instrument. "You go," he said to Katie. "And thanks."

"I'll see you later, Jonty. 'Bye, Ellie." Katie shot them both a grin and jogged down the beach.

"Hi there," Ellie chirped as she crouched down. The poor little boy seemed scared stiff, or cripplingly shy. "Your daddy tells me your name's Jonty," she said brightly. "It's nice to meet you, Jonty. What do you think Santa Claus might bring you next week? I'm really hoping he brings me a new boogie board."

Still the little boy stood motionless, staring at her with liquid blue eyes.

Cy turned to her, his face etched with grief. "Ellie, Jonty has selective mutism. He doesn't speak."

2

———

$\mathcal{C}$y scanned Ellie's face for a reaction and locked a response in his chest. His throat dried as silence wrapped around them, thick and terrible.

He could tell by the tilt of someone's head whether they felt pity for his son, or suspicious about why a six-year-old couldn't or wouldn't speak.

Ellie took off her sunglasses, knelt down, and picked up a perfect white shell from the glittering sand. As she held it flat in her palm and lifted her face, Cy could've hugged her for the way she looked at his boy, her eyes shining with kindness. This wasn't the girl he'd remembered; she was something altogether different. Captivating, radiant, with a presence that drew him close. He couldn't keep his eyes off her. The tension he'd carried for months slipped from his shoulders. He could do this. *They* could do this. But he had to ask her in the right moment.

Her voice, low and musical, pulled him to the present. "Can you hear me, Jonty?" Staring at the sand, his son chewed his lip and Cy stilled as he waited for a reaction. It was so important that this first meeting between them was a positive one.

Cy's belly pulled tight and he looked from Jonty to Ellie and nodded in reply to her question, desperate not to break the spell as he watched the tiniest of frowns scar the pale skin between her eyebrows. He drew a deeper breath. God, she was beautiful, and so absolutely the right person to help them. If everything went well, maybe he could win her back for good?

She looked at his son intently. "You know something really amazing?" Her face again broke into a sunny smile. "Your daddy and I used to play on this beach when we were small. Probably right where we're standing now." With a slender finger, she gently brushed sand from the shell. "We'd meet down here after breakfast and build huts from driftwood, or make castles with towers and moats. And one of our very favorite things to do was find shells and listen to the sound of the sea." She paused in mock concentration as she lifted the shell to her ear. "Hey, we might've picked up this very same shell all those years ago."

Jonty's eyes flicked up at her and a hole drilled deep in Cy's chest. *Please let this work.*

"Would you like to listen, Jonty?"

Holding out the shell again, she moved as if to get closer to his damaged child, to let a little boy from the city hear the ocean in the shell's cool, hollow depths. But instead of his son's face lighting up, instead of him racing forward and reaching for the shell and eagerly putting it to his ear, Jonty turned in a wild arc and ran back to the house, his hair shivering in the wind, the scarf like a frenzied snake whipping out behind him.

Cy forced his legs to stay rigid as blood pumped cold through his veins. He struggled to hold still and not sprint after his son. To not call and try to comfort as he'd done so many times before. It only ever made it worse. Jonty would be ready to form a relationship with Ellie in his own time, but they only had two weeks until they had to be back in Colorado. There was so much at stake, but forcing the issue wouldn't help.

"Oh, no!" Ellie's voice dipped as she stood and clutched the shell to her chest. "I'm so sorry."

He took a step forward as her eyes widened, face ashen.

"I didn't mean to—"

He put his hand on her waist and awareness flooded him as the warmth of her skin seeped through her woolen jacket. It was the first time he'd touched her since he'd arrived. He should've hugged her tight when he'd seen her again, not treated her like a stranger, but this new sense of her made him hesitate. She was still distant, and he needed to tread carefully. "It wasn't you," he said.

"I hope not, but I still feel awful. Should you go to him? He looked terrified."

"I will in a minute. When he's caught his breath and calmed down." He clenched his fingers into his palm, the pain of blunt fingernails comforting. "He's had the same sort of reaction a hundred times before, and if I don't respond properly, it can be a disaster. If I go to him too quickly, he gets more anxious. I stop myself from picking him up and hugging him, telling him it'll be all right. I have to wait until he's ready. He has the physical ability to talk and will when he feels completely safe." The words fell heavy from his mouth, sterile and rehearsed, so she couldn't hear what the condition truly meant for him. "Sometimes, when it's just the two of us, and then only a couple of words. But most of the time he can't speak.

It's not that he doesn't want to, it's that in many situations he can't. Jonty hasn't spent much time with me since he was born, but I'm hoping to get custody from his grandparents now."

"Oh, Cy. That must be so difficult."

He couldn't bring himself to look at her, afraid of what she might see if he did. A father terrified he'd screw his son's life up even more. He tensed muscles, ready for more questions, but he had to tell her all this so she'd understand why he'd come here, why he needed her help. He shrugged, but the tension in his shoulders was bolted on. "His doctor wants to begin a new regime of treatment."

"Is that why you came here? For a vacation before the treatment starts?"

She looked up at him, and he almost told her the truth, but now wasn't the time. Tonight, when it could be just the two of them, without distractions. That's when he'd ask her. "Something like that."

She took a step toward him, and for a minute he thought she might hug him. The call of her body was as fresh as it had been that one perfect afternoon eight years ago, and he couldn't let himself be distracted. Ellie had to trust him now.

He scanned the shoreline and let the hypnotic rhythm of the waves slow his body. "I hope I can always bring him here."

"Cy...I..." She trapped a lip between her teeth and reached out to him. "You will be able to, now the restoration's happening."

He turned to face her and her hand fell away. "Do you have time to go through some of it?"

She tilted her head and frowned a little. "Now's not the time to talk about the project," she said quietly. "We can get together later."

"When?"

"When you've settled in. After Christmas, maybe."

"How about tonight?"

Her forehead tightened before she spoke. "Okay, where shall we meet? The Blue Tui?"

"I can't leave Jonty," he said. "Can you come to my place? After eight, when he's asleep."

She paused for a moment. "Okay, I'll see you then."

Ellie: *Oh, I'm so glad the dinner went well, Kirin!*

Ellie sat at the Starfish kitchen table, so thankful she could keep up her regular online chats with the girls she'd met through an online life coaching course. In the early days, they'd skip the workshops they were supposed to be attending and just secretly chat for the allotted hour, but now they jumped online every few days to check in with each other. Even though they'd never met, these girls knew more about her deepest hopes and dreams than almost anyone, and she loved them to death.

Kirin: A-FREAKING -MAZING! *God, it felt so good to be back in a commercial kitchen, and the feedback about the food was incredible!*

Gwin: *Go you! I'm so happy for you, Kirin. This has been such a tough road, but now you can kick those non-believers to the curb!*

Ellie: *And Makeover Man? Was the Beautiful Blake pleased with the way things went? I bet there were some celebrations.*

Kirin: *You could say he was. . .pleased. . .There might have been a bit of celebration action in a store cupboard after the dinner. . .but my lips are sealed!*

Gwin: *LOLOL!! Oh that's so good, I'm really happy things are going so well for you guys. Ellie, how are things in New*

Zealand? I so wish I was on a beach right now. Hope you've got a pink drink in hand with an umbrella in it.

Ellie's fingers hovered above the keyboard. Did she really want to tell these gorgeous women how she was feeling? Like she'd stepped back in time eight years and could still remember the feel of Cy under her fingertips. The way he'd whispered her name.

She always tried to be positive and upbeat with them, but they'd all helped Kirin through a tough time, and they'd communicated often enough by now to know she could trust them.

Ellie: *Remember that old flame I sent the meeting info to? Well, he turned up.*

Kirin: *From the States, right? I'm picking the reunion was awkward as all hell?*

Ellie: *Awkward on steroids. A hall full of people all listening to me talk. He arrives late. I blush to the tips of my toenails and make a deal with the devil for the ground to swallow me whole.*

Gwin: *And did you get that achy feeling? Like you know it's history, but when you look at him, you can remember the sweet smell of his skin...*

Kirin: *And you remember the cute way he used to look at you...*

Ellie: *God, yes, all of it. And we ended up going back to my beach house.*

Kirin: *And you jumped his bones and want us to tell you that you shouldn't regret it for a second?!!!!*

Ellie: *How about he introduced me to his son who's six and can't talk, and who I scared the living daylights out of. And that he's all serious now and seems really intent on interrogating me about the project.*

Gwin: *Oh, wow, poor kid?!*

Kirin: *Does Hunka-First-Love have a wife or a girlfriend?*

Ellie: *I get the feeling he doesn't. It's nice to see him and everything, but we didn't part in the best way and we haven't been in touch at all in the last eight years, so it is pretty awkward.*

Gwin: *Why can't his son talk?*

Ellie: *I'm not really sure what Jonty's issue is yet, but Cy's asked me to come over tonight so he can talk to me about the project. Maybe he'll tell me a little more then.*

Gwin: *Feel like telling us what happened all those years ago? How you guys broke up, I mean.*

Ellie rolled her lips together. No, she didn't need to tell them the whole tragic story. The bare bones would be enough.

Ellie: *It's not an original plot! We were childhood best friends. Mostly in holidays when we'd come to our neighboring beach houses. When we turned eighteen, we got hot and heavy one afternoon and did the wild thing. He was my first. I told him how I really felt about him and then the next day, he took off.*

Kirin: *Ouch! Those first heartbreaks sure are the most brutal. You know my old advice would be to get him out of your system for good by having a summer fling, but with a little boy around—especially one who has issues—that's probably a bad idea.*

Gwin: *What do you feel like doing, Ellie?*

Ellie: *In all honesty, I'd really just like to avoid him for the next few weeks, but it's a tight little community here. We have beach cricket on Christmas Day and a community pageant on New Year's Eve . . . If I avoid him, it's going to be really obvious.*

Gwin: *Oh, I forgot that you guys have a summer Christmas.*

Kirin: *But you're busy, right? You have work to do, so that's a good excuse.*

Ellie: *That's true.*

Kirin: *And a couple of weeks ago you said your sister and nephew would be at the beach house with you, right? Maybe* *your sister can help to keep you away from him. I bet she has an opinion about what happened...*

Ellie: *Yeah, Fleur knows Cy really well too, of course, but she knows the way things ended and that I haven't seen him since.*

Gwin: *Any other prospective summer flings? There's just something about a kiwi or an Aussie guy that makes me all hot and bothered. I'm thinking Chris Hemsworth or Martin Henderson.*

Ellie: *Doubt it! This is a really family orientated place. So hardly any singles. People have been coming for generations, so it's big families all together in the holiday houses for Christmas, community events, that sort of thing.*

Kirin: *And I know you've been worried about pulling this whole project off, so you're going to want to keep a pretty professional profile.*

Ellie: *That's right. Oh man, I wish I didn't have to go over to his place tonight. Jonty didn't have a great time with the sitter today and he'll be asleep, so...*

Kirin: *So you keep it completely professional. Drop a few things like how successful you are as a landscape architect, how there's a guy in every port and isn't it funny how dramatic we are as teenagers.*

Ellie: *You're right. We were young and naïve back then. He obviously has a lot going on in his life and so do I. No one should ever imagine getting back with their first love, should they?*

Gwin: *Nothing wrong with imagining! He'll probably just want to question you about where his septic tank should go or what he doesn't like about your plan.*

They went on chatting for a while, Ellie telling them all the things she was looking forward to about a New Zealand Christmas Day, Gwin sharing her exciting plans for moving away from her hometown and the tough times she's had there. Kirin was on cloud nine about her relationship with her image stylist, Blake, and they ended the call laughing about all the new places Kirin and he could make out in a commercial kitchen.

When she'd signed off the call, Ellie smiled as she looked out to the waves gently breaking on the beach. Of course it made sense that she'd been a little uncomfortable at seeing Cy again, but Gwin and Kirin were right—what they'd had had clearly been one sided, and everyone knew that rekindling an old flame was never a good idea.

When Cy opened the door later that evening, Ellie stood on the bottom step. A kick of heat punched through his body, the unfamiliar sensation shocking him. Unlike earlier, her hair was a loose cloud around her shoulders, and the dark suit had been replaced by a white sundress that showcased the honey tan of her skin. An orange cardigan was tied at her waist and she held a plate of brightly colored cupcakes in one hand, a briefcase in the other.

"What do you know about wounded pukeko chicks?" he said. "Jonty's asleep, but I promised I'd ask as soon as you got here."

"A little." She rose on tiptoe to peer into the cardboard box he was holding, and a scent of spring flowers and sunshine filled his senses. "Isn't he beautiful? Where'd you find him?"

He breathed her in again before she stepped back. "Jonty and I found him lolloping around the house. Seems he's done something to one of his toes. There's a bit of a tear on his skin." The swamp hen scratched in the bottom of the box, its inky-black feathers fluffed around it like a tutu, its enormous wading feet slithering. Cy led Ellie inside. "I told Jonty if anyone knew how to look after a chick, you would."

"He's a long way from home," she said. "Pukekos usually stay off the beach. Maybe give him some bread and milk, keep the box covered, so it's dark." She walked to the kitchen and put the plate on the counter. "Fleur sent some Cranberry Carol Cupcakes from her store."

"Thanks, J will love them. You can put your things down anywhere."

"The chick won't survive around here too long with all those grouchy seagulls, especially if he's cut. It might be a good idea to take it out to the marshy bit by the highway when you've treated its foot. We fixed up a weka that had been caught in a rattrap once. What sort of first-aid kit do you have? We might find some eucalyptus oil to clean the cut, at least."

He lifted a shoulder. "Don't know. It's been so long since I've been here. Let's look in the bathroom cupboard. Mum used to keep stuff in there."

They made their way to the tiny bathroom. He'd hesitated when Jonty had shown him the chick, but it was the first thing his little boy had taken any interest in since they'd arrived, and he wanted to do what he could for it. He bent down to a bottom cupboard and tugged at the door.

"The green basin and tub!" Ellie exclaimed.

Cy turned, a smile digging into his cheeks. "Pure seventies style. Mum wanted to redesign in here, but Kelly and I wouldn't let her. There's something special about taking a bath in a deep green tub."

She tucked a piece of hair behind her ear and leaned closer to a shelf. "And you still have that little fish skeleton we found on Paige's Point! That must be fifteen years old."

He looked back into the cupboard. "Don't know if

there'll be anything useful in here." He stood and handed her a raggedy bag and she unzipped it, then riffled through, shaking her head. "We can't use any of these things. They'll be too strong on his delicate skin. I think I have something back in the shed at Starfish."

"Could you bring it tomorrow? And then maybe you could help us release the chick? I'd really appreciate it."

Their gazes met, and in a beat of silence, his breath stalled. Where had the years gone? The lazy days when all he'd had to worry about was catching the next wave, not how he could survive without his son. "It's great to see you again, Ellie. I'm sorry we lost touch."

She ran her tongue across her bottom lip and shifted against the bathroom vanity. "A lot of water under the bridge since then." She cast a glance at the doorway.

"Do you think about it much?" he asked quietly as he leaned against the wall. "Those times?" They'd barely spoken about their life before. He could hardly ask her to become his wife when the terrible elephant was still suffocating them in the corner of the room.

She breathed deep then blew out softly. "Of course. A lot happened in my life back then and it took me a long time to work through everything."

"This time of year must be really hard."

She blinked, and her eyes glistened. "William died on the twenty-eighth of December. I can still remember the way the sun scorched my skin, the sound of the breakers after the storm, the way the sand trapped my feet when I started running to him. It should've been such a perfect summer's day."

He nodded, his chest tightening at the memory. If it still hurt when *he* thought about that day, what must it be like for her? For her whole family?

She held her hand in her hair. "I can still remember the way Mum's body locked when the paramedic told her William was dead. Sort of broken, as if all her bones had come loose. I can't smell that brand of sunscreen without wanting to vomit."

"Does coming here make it harder for you?"

She blinked and smiled widely. "No. I've learned to accept the terrible times with the great times. They're all memories to cherish because they've made me who I am. I love coming back here. Couldn't imagine not having Rata Cove in my life."

She spoke with the power of someone who'd learned to find the beauty in life again.

"How about Fleur? How does she cope?"

"It's different for her. She wasn't there. Wasn't responsible like I was."

"Like *we* were."

"No." Her tone was definite. "Not *we*."

He remembered how they'd made William promise to stay making sandcastles, said they'd be back soon. And while her little brother was chasing after his hat that had blown off into the water, they'd been having sex on his father's yacht, oblivious to the tragedy unfolding only meters away. William's safety had been just as much his responsibility as it was Ellie's. If he hadn't been so focused on making love to her, it would all have been different.

"Did you want to ask me something more about the restoration? I can't stay long. I'd sit with Louis while Fleur goes out to visit friends."

"I do have a few questions. Let's go through to the living room."

When they'd moved back into the other room, he offered her a glass of wine.

She sat down at the huge table. "Thanks." She unlatched the briefcase. "I've brought some plans for you to look through. I've told everyone I'm open to submissions until the end of next week, but I won't be working Christmas day, of course. What are your plans for Christmas dinner? You're welcome to come to Starfish."

He poured a glass of golden wine, passed it, and pulled up a chair beside her. His stomach pulled in a sharp knot and he cleared his throat.

He shook his head and clasped his hands together on the table. The stubble on his chin had grown darker since this afternoon and made him look like a casually elegant movie star. "I haven't given much thought to Christmas Day, to be honest."

She searched Cy's face. He looked more strained than yesterday, as if the weight of the world was gradually wearing him down. Maybe it was the conversation they'd just had in the bathroom, but she was glad they'd acknowledged the past. It might be years before she saw Cy again, and besides, it was Christmastime. She would never, ever get over the death of her little brother, and would never forgive herself who the circumstances, but she had long ago given herself permission to go forward and live a life that would have made her brother proud.

"We'd love to have you at our house for Christmas dinner if you think it's something Jonty would like. We can show him a real New Zealand beach Christmas, strawberries and pavlova and a swim in the sea after lunch. What do you say?"

"Ellie." He put his hand on hers and sparks flew up her

arm. His jaw had tightened, and a muscle danced under the skin. There was something powerful, almost frightening, in his eyes. "I need your help."

"My help?" The crease on his forehead deepened, and she played with the pen in front of her. "Sure, if I can. What do you need?"

He pushed the chair back and stood. "We were great friends once, right? You knew me pretty well."

The look in his bright blue eyes hooked her. He shoved a hand through his hair. Was he nervous? "You were the only one who knew about Dad's cheating and how much it was destroying our family and you supported me through that."

There'd been days when Cy wouldn't say anything, but she knew his father and mother had been fighting. He'd disappear for hours and hours, sometimes having surfed all day; other days, he never said where he'd been. He'd just take off.

"Even though things became complicated at the end, for the most part we've been able to talk about anything with each other, right?"

She nodded.

He turned and faced her completely. Excitement, fear, *something* raced through his eyes. "There's something I need from you, Ellie. Something I can't get from anyone else." His head bowed, his hand gripping the wineglass before he lifted his face to her again. "Ellie. I need to marry you."

3

—————

*V*ertigo rushed at her, and she gripped the side of the table. Surely she'd misheard. "Marry me?"

He leaned in as if every scrap of energy was going into this proposal. His eyes had darkened and held her still. "Jonty's mom died a year ago and her parents want their custody arrangement to become permanent. They've been his guardians since he was born, so they have a very good case." His tone became more insistent. "I've spent six years without my son, and I won't let another day go by when he's not with me."

Before she could reply, he rushed on. "I need you to help me convince the authorities, and Susan's parents, that Jonty should be with me."

Ellie wiped her cool palms down her cheeks. That poor little boy had no mommy? The thought chipped at her heart. And why hadn't Cy been in his son's life? The horror of what he and Jonty were going through bit deep, but after everything that had happened between them, and the fact they hadn't seen each other in eight years, how could Cy possibly expect her to agree to something so outrageous?

Her tongue dried in her mouth, but she had to know more. "What happened? Why hasn't Jonty been with you?"

He shook his bowed head for a second, then looked back at her with glassy eyes. "We hadn't been living together for a long time when Susan died a year ago from a drug overdose."

"Oh, Cy, I'm so sorry."

His chest moved as he breathed deep. "We met at a surf and snow show when she was training for the Olympics. Jonty wasn't planned and the fact that she had to put her training on hold during the pregnancy had a huge impact on her. She had serious postpartum depression after Jonty was born and didn't want a relationship with me anymore. We were only together a few months before she got pregnant, but I'd always thought we could make a go of it

"I hoped if I gave her some space it might help her heal, but she said I'd never see Jonty, that he'd never know I was his father and that she'd told her parents I'd abandoned her. I didn't want to make things harder for her in the state she was in, so I took a step back, thinking things would be different when she got better."

"And did she?" Her question was probing, but she was desperate to know what he'd been through, what had changed him from the confident and relaxed teenager she'd fallen for to the coiled man who sat beside her now.

He blew out a sharp breath. "Susan was okay for a couple of years while she was on medication. She'd move around a lot, so I had to keep tracking her down and even though she wouldn't let me see Jonty, I managed to get her mother to speak to me, give me progress reports. Maria was keeping a close eye on Susan too." He curled the fingers of one hand around his wrist. "But when Jonty went to kindergarten, Susan went off her medication. Things disintegrated.

She told a friend that she shouldn't feel depressed anymore. That she had to get back to snowboarding, pick up where she left off and of course she couldn't do that with the drugs."

The truth of what had happened lay in the lines that deepened around his eyes and in the blanch of skin as he pressed fingers into his flesh. "I'd heard that she was leaving him more and more with her parents, as she wasn't coping. I was preparing a case for at least shared custody when—"

He rested his head in his hands for a moment, and she held her breath before he pulled his eyes to hers. "I got a call from her mother when I was in Baja. Jonty had waited outside the gates when school finished but Susan never came."

The skin of his throat moved in tight, sharp swallows before he continued. "The school couldn't track anyone down until six o'clock in the evening and even then they had trouble getting him to move from the gate." His voice shook and Ellie moved closer and gently put her hand on his arm, every cell in her body aching for him, wanting to comfort and be close just the way he'd been with her after William died. She breathed over the hardening lump in her throat.

He carried on, but his voice got quieter. "She died at home from a drug overdose. She'd always told Jonty to wait at the gate and not move until she came for him. But she never did..." Breath rasped out of him. "She couldn't get back to professional boarding, her friends had moved on, Jonty had gone to school. Even her relationship with her parents had broken down."

"Oh, Cy." Ellie inched closer and before she knew it, the rigid muscles under his shirt heated her palm as she stroked his arm. His ragged breaths drilled into her and she willed his grief away.

He sat up swiftly, rubbing his palms across his face, and her hand dropped from his arm. Strength seemed to shoot into him as his spine straightened and his chin lifted. "That was a year ago." He cleared his throat before continuing. "Until a few weeks ago, Jonty wanted to stay at that gate every afternoon, as if being there would bring his mother back. I had to get him away from the constant reminders. To a safe place." Ellie looked down as his hand made a slow fist.

"So what's the custody situation now?"

His fist stayed tight, his eyes fixed on it. "Even though I've had access to him since she died, Susan's parents want full custody."

A lump rose in Ellie's throat. "And you're disputing it?"

As he lifted his gaze to her, the determination in his eyes was electric. "It's time my son and I were together. I want them in his life and I'll never stop them seeing their grand-son, but I'll fight them for my son."

Ellie shook her head as she tried to make sense of every-thing. "Is that why Jonty doesn't speak? Because of the trauma he's been through?" Her heart thumped heavily. She'd never seen Cy like this, so fragile and full of grief, and it tore at her.

"It's part of it. But it's a lot more complex than Susan's death alone. The doctor thinks he'd been affected by Susan's depression all along, by the fact his world was frac-tured." He shot her a look of desperation and leaned away, his dark eyes wide and endless, and she knew that feeling like it was part of her heart.

"Will he be able to speak again?" She moved forward. It was as if Cy's story had cast a spell over her.

"He speaks now when he feels completely safe and secure. And that's my mission, to provide him with a life of security and fun and laughter. No more sadness, no more grief. I want him to have fun, to feel alive, to be a child." His gaze held her until her eyes ached. "Jonty's improved a lot since he's been seeing Doctor Marlowe. He's a world authority on selective mutism. He thinks he can do a lot when we get back."

Cy lifted his chin, and the determination on his perfect face was electric. "It's time my son and I were together, Ellie. I really feel for Susan's parents, of course I do, but Jonty should be with me now, and the only person who can help me with that is you. I need you, Ellie. *We* need you. You and I had something once. Maybe we can find that again. I miss you, believe it or not. It'd be good to have you in my life again, if even for a short while."

Shaken by everything he'd said, she focused on the table and tried to hide the tangle of emotion inside her. "So, let me get this straight. You think that being married will help you win custody of Jonty? You think taking me to the States as your pretend wife will show the courts you'll be a better father?"

"Yes. No." He nodded, then shook his head. "I mean, we'd be really married. You'd be my wife." He touched her shoulder so she was forced to look at him. "I know this is a crazy request, Ellie. It's selfish, and it's out of the blue. I know you've got a full life, but I promise the fake marriage wouldn't be for long, just until I'm awarded custody and then a decent length of time until everything settles. A year, tops."

She pulled in a breath and bit her lip, unable to believe he'd really thought this was possible.

He gently squeezed her shoulder. "You asked me to do

something once and although it went against everything I believed in, I did it for you, Ellie. I'm asking for the favor to be returned. I'm desperate."

She laid her palms flat on the table and tried to steady her breathing. "I can't believe you'd ask me to do this. After the way you left me when I needed you most, the way you just walked...no...*ran* out of my life when we should've been there for each other. I can't believe you'd ask something so outrageous of me now."

He sat back as if she'd slapped him, a look of confusion rippling across his features. "I know I didn't handle it well, but I had to leave back then so you could focus on your family's grief, not me and the secret you were so desperate we keep."

She softened her voice, trying to imagine how desperate he must be to have to ask her, of all people. "I'm so sorry for the situation you're in, heartbroken for Jonty, and sad that you feel there's no other way around this, but you've got to see that I can't possibly do this, Cy. I live and work all around the world, and I have projects lined up for the next twelve months. And besides all of that, I'm not good with children. The last person you need around Jonty is someone who doesn't know what they're doing."

His Adam's apple moved as he swallowed, and then he shook his head. "Ellie, I'm sorry. I'm so sorry. I understand this is a shock, but I've run out of options and when your letter came and I thought back to how generous you've always been, how caring..." His voice ran out to nothing and she had to stop herself from covering his strong hand with hers. "When you asked me to lie about what really happened the day William died, I tried to talk you round. But when I saw how much it meant to you to spare your parents more anguish, I realized it would hurt you more if I told the truth. You asked me to keep that secret, and I did, Ellie. For eight years. Now I'm asking you to do something that will limit the hurt for me and my son. I owed it to myself, and to Jonty, to at least give it a shot by asking you."

Her heart looped. He was right. He had kept their secret, despite being dead against it. Fleur had had a baby at eighteen, and her parents had always made Ellie promise to be careful. She'd been anything but and had been desperate not to cause them any more pain. But it was Cy running away that still made her blood run cold. Besides, she didn't like his assumption that her life was so uneventful that she could simply drop everything and fit into his. "What if I'm already married?"

"Kelly mentioned you weren't." He shifted his weight in the chair, at least having the grace to look uncomfortable that he'd checked with his sister.

"I could have a boyfriend. Someone serious who might be affected by you asking me this."

He threw her a skin-tingling grin. "You're right. I'm sorry, I should have asked. *Do* you have a boyfriend?"

"No," she said, trying to avoid the heated look in his eyes. She chewed her lip and clasped her hands together. "Is the situation really as desperate as you think it is? Courts give custody to sole parents all the time. Why would you need a wife, or a partner?"

He nodded. "That's true, but because I haven't had the chance to be fully involved in Jonty's life, the court, not to mention Susan's parents, would look far more favorably on me if I was married and settled than if I'm a single business owner who travels for a living as I have been doing."

Feeling numb with confusion, each of his words swirled in her head and she let all the thoughts trapped there fall from her mouth. "But a wife, Cy. That should be someone you've developed a relationship with, someone who you're committed to." *Breathe.* "God, Cy, someone you *love*?"

"Of *course*," he said, his face softening with a smile. "In an ideal world, I'd love to provide Jonty with those things, but time's run out. We have no other options."

"But why *me*? Don't you know someone in the States who could do this? Why come all the way here and ask me?" Because he thought she owed him?

"Although Susan's father's American, her mother's a New Zealander — Susan picked my accent, that's how we first got talking. Anyway, her parents had planned to move back to Auckland. If I have a New Zealand wife, they'll be less likely to feel they'll lose touch with Jonty when they move here. It might make them feel less like they'd be shut out of his life."

She shook her head, and his tone grew more intense. "I'm his father and I love him more than my own life. It can't turn out any other way. I've got to do whatever I can to have permanent custody of my son. If that means having a sham marriage to get things started, then I'm prepared to do it. A sham marriage with you is more real than a sham marriage with someone I don't have any history with. Can't you see that?"

This was insane, but no matter how many times she swallowed, the band around her throat wouldn't release. She had to keep talking, give herself time to make sense of it. "But what if I said yes and came to America and you lose anyway?"

His face slackened. "It wouldn't happen. If I can prove I have a stable life, that I am a good father, I'll have my son for good. It's not that I want to prevent his grandparents from having access. I just can't settle for anything less than full custody of my son."

"And what about Jonty?" She focused on his forehead, anywhere but directly in his eyes. Her heart shrank at the thought of that little boy and the enormous changes he'd go through if he were to have a temporary mother.

"What do you mean?"

"Have you told him your plan? Does he know you want to marry me?"

"I haven't told him yet. I wanted to give him a chance to get to know you first."

"And that hasn't exactly gone swimmingly, has it?"

He blew out a breath. "No, but given time..."

"I don't have time to get to know him, Cy. You're here for two weeks and then gone again, and you saw what a disaster our first meeting was. I'm not cut out to be responsible for children."

Cell-deep, her answer was no. No, because it was dishonest to Jonty, no because it went against everything she believed about marriage and commitment, and no because Cy had hurt her once, he'd broken her heart, and she wouldn't let him do it again.

She opened her mouth to speak, but her shoulders sagged. "I don't—"

He held his hand in a stop sign and smiled. "Of course this is a huge thing for you to contemplate. Just think about it. Take a couple of days if you need to. I know it's outrageous ... completely crazy... but I really believe it'll work and you're the only one I can ask. The only person who knows me well enough to pull this off." He smiled softly.

She picked up her briefcase, her heart still beating hollow in her chest. "I need to go."

"But you'll come by in the morning?"

She looked at him, puzzled.

"Help release the pukeko chick. Jonty's worried about it

being lost, that its mother won't know where it is. I told him you rescued more beached jellyfish and tide-stranded crabs than anyone I know."

What it was she didn't know, but something in his eyes, something achingly familiar in his voice, made Ellie hesitate for just a moment so that she couldn't back out when he spoke again.

"So you'll come?"

Before she could stop herself, she nodded, knowing full well that spending more time with Cy Hathaway and his little boy was going to cause the feelings already germinating in her heart to dig deeper by the day.

"And as for the marriage. I'd like to know your decision soon," he said. "Before Christmas if possible." His voice was gentle. "And we'd love to take you up on your offer for Christmas Day."

She pushed her chair back and stood, her hands still trembling, regretting that she'd asked about Christmas Day, regretting she'd come here tonight at all. "Surely there's a better solution, Cy. Maybe there's more you can do to build a good case for custody. Something less. . .drastic."

He breathed deep, his mouth set in a line. "If I can't come up with something bulletproof, I'll lose my son. We need you, Ellie."

She pushed her chair in as her mind jumped ahead and the ramifications of what he'd asked of her snowballed. She ran her tongue across her lips as a cloak of responsibility settled over her, the weight dragging on her body. But what if pretending to be a happily married couple could ensure Jonty's happiness? "I'll think about it."

Cy paced the next morning, from the kitchen to the deck and back again. He wondered if she'd show, if she'd be late, and if she'd have a decision yet.

As soon as she'd left last night, he'd wanted to call her back, say how sorry he was that he'd had to ask this of her. All the old feelings of their friendship had returned, but with them came a stirring he couldn't ignore, a connection he wanted to revisit.

He was glad he'd told her everything last night. The minute he'd seen the recognition in her face, the understanding of losing someone so suddenly and shockingly, hope had surged through him.

He wanted Jonty to like her, not to run away as he'd done yesterday, but to see her as the wonderful, caring person she was. If his plan worked as he hoped, she was going to play a big part in Jonty's life in the next few months, and he really wanted them to get along.

Jonty was waiting too, sitting on the deck in his Hawaiian shorts, yellow t-shirt and purple sneakers. The cardboard box containing the pukeko was balanced on his knee, the bright linen tea towel and his scarf over the top of it as he looked up the beach. And Cy wished he'd explained to Ellie how important it was that she be on time.

"How's he doing?" Cy asked his son as he made the trek back across the deck again. With a pudgy hand, Jonty lifted the cloth and peered underneath. When he looked up, he just nodded, then went back to looking up the beach.

Cy saw her first. She was walking with someone he guessed was Fleur. A lanky young boy slouched behind them.

Unlike yesterday, Ellie's hair was now loose around her shoulders and the dark suit had been replaced by shorts and a t-shirt that clung to her torso, accentuating the parts of her that were so new to him, the soft curve of her breasts, the mature line of her hips. A kick of heated desire punched through his body, the unfamiliar sensation shocking him.

He leaned against the railing and was raked by a sudden sadness. He'd thrown away Ellie's friendship. As he watched her getting closer, her head down, arms swinging gently by her sides, he remembered being so close. But close like a friend, not like the boyfriend she'd wanted.

He'd done everything he could to help her after William's death, keeping her busy, away from her parents' sadness. She'd thought it was something more, and he'd responded when she'd kissed him. Oh, he'd wanted her then. And the feel of her sun kissed skin against his had driven him wild like he hadn't expected and they'd made love. But then she'd said she loved him and it was all too much. She'd been a friend he needed to take care of and he couldn't do that anymore.

"Hi!" she called as she opened the small white gate that separated the lawn from the beach and the three of them walked through.

"Cy!" Fleur rushed toward him. "How amazing to see you again! And this must be your little boy!"

He leaned close and hugged Ellie's sister. He'd always liked Fleur, but she'd never hung around with him and Ellie much. She'd never seemed to like the cove and was always going backwards and forwards to parties in the city. Fleur wasn't an adventurous daredevil like her little sister and when she'd been lost in the bush for a week once with his friend Jake, it had really affected her. She and Jake had been rescued about the time of his last visit here, and he hadn't seen her since.

"This is my son, Louis," she said, and the boy threw him a lopsided grin. "We're off to the camp store but just thought we'd stop by and say hi. What are you doing for Christmas?" she asked. "Ellie says your parents and Kelly aren't here, so why don't you—"

"We should get going, Cy," Ellie said as she moved toward the house. "I'll see you back home for lunch, Fleur?"

Fleur shrugged her shoulders, and with a wink just for Cy, turned to go. "Okay, sweetie. Nice to see you again, Cy. Maybe we can catch up at the New Year's pageant or something?"

"Sure," he said, surprised she was leaving so quickly.

"See you later, Cy. See you back at the house, Ellie."

"Hi Jonty," Ellie said when her sister had gone. "How's our little friend doing today?"

Jonty stayed where he was but pulled the tea towel and scarf back so she could peer inside.

"Did you feed him this morning?"

He nodded.

Cy grinned. At least she hadn't been put off by his son's reaction to her yesterday

She glanced at her watch. "Shall we get going? I thought we could just drive to one of the paddocks by the highway. There are always pukeko hens there."

"Go and get some shoes on, J." Cy said. "You don't want bare feet where we're going." The little boy just sat still. "Jonty, I said go and get your shoes, please."

When Jonty didn't respond a second time, but instead put his head back under the tea towel, Cy threw Ellie a helpless look. "I won't be a minute."

When they were in the car, Cy drove in silence. From the rear vision mirror, he watched Jonty in his booster seat, the box on his lap and his head permanently under the tea towel. He sometimes didn't know how hard to push his son, when to make allowances that his boy hardly knew him, when to recognize that disobedience and tantrums were part of being six and not because your whole life had been turned upside down. He gripped the steering wheel tighter. It wasn't right that he second guessed himself on everything, wasn't right that he couldn't make his son better just by loving him.

A little way out of the cove, Cy drew the car alongside a post-and-wire fence and they got out. Native bush circled wide green fields and the familiar call of the native birds in the distance was comforting.

"There's a creek along that side of the paddock," Ellie said as she pulled the wire wide to let Jonty through. "It comes under the road from the cove and can make the paddock quite marshy." She held a hand up to shade her eyes. "I can't see any pukekos, though. Let's look."

She led the way and Cy's pulse nudged up a notch as he tried not to watch the way her hips swayed in her khaki shorts as she walked. The white t-shirt hugged her small waist and her flip-flops made sucking noises in the damp grass. She might be twenty-seven, but the way she moved, loose limbed and supple, made her look years younger.

"This should be a great place for the chick," she said to Jonty. He looked straight ahead, the box held out in front of him. "Pukekos like to hang out in groups, so when we find some adults we should be able to leave him with them and he'll be—" She stopped abruptly at a dip in the earth.

"What is it?" Cy drew closer and then stopped speaking as he realized what they were looking at. This wasn't the creek he'd remembered as a kid, the sparkling water running over white stones. This was brown and brackish with a yellow foam at its edges.

"It's no wonder there aren't any pukekos here," Ellie said simply as she knelt down. "This creek's polluted."

Everything she'd said at the meeting about the health of the cove, leaking septic tanks and unchecked rubbish, came flooding back.

Jonty looked up at him with those haunted brown eyes, and Cy knew what he was thinking. "We won't leave the little guy here by himself, bud. We'll have to find where all the mom and dad pukekos have gone, but until we do, I think he could stay with us. We need to get his toe better anyway."

He shot a look at Ellie.

Something new moved across her face before she spoke. "I'll do a bit of investigating as to where they might be, but I think he'll be in really good hands if you're looking after him, Jonty." She tilted her chin so she was looking directly into his eyes. "He'll need to live in a pukeko family eventually, but we certainly don't want to leave him here all by himself."

A smile lit the little boy's face and sent a warm wallop to Cy's chest. He grinned back as he picked the box up from the grass and put it back in his son's hands. "You take the box back to the car Jonty while I have a talk to Ellie about where those moms and dads might be."

He watched his son move across the paddock and bend down to examine something. The brilliant green grass was dotted with wild daisies and dandelions, everything new and potentially exciting for his son. His chest staggered and his throat tightened as it always did when he thought about everything his little boy had lost.

"I'm kinda glad we didn't find the pukekos," he said while they watched Jonty.

"Why?" She looked up at him, the sun on her face.

"He got up at six this morning to see how the chick was doing and I've never seen him so interested in anything."

Her slow smile threaded a string of warmth through him as he hurried on. "He's never had a pet because Susan was in an apartment. It'd be nice for him to have something to focus on in the next few days."

Christmas was in a few days. He'd tried to pretend it wasn't happening, but the decorations had been in the shops before they'd left, so Jonty knew it wasn't far away. Perhaps being summer they could avoid it somehow.

He wanted to turn back time at this part of the year, run away to when he was ten or eleven and nothing was more important than winning a game of beach cricket or catching the next wave.

"What about Susan's family? Didn't they want to spend Christmas with Jonty?" Ellie whispered.

"They agreed to me bringing him here. It'll show they're sympathetic to my position, but I think they're secretly hoping it'll be tough for me. That I'll go back ready for them to take over."

"So, you'll definitely stay in the States when the case is over?" She stopped walking and her golden eyes pulled at him.

He hesitated for a moment before turning to look at her, remembering what she'd said about wanting to always come here. How he'd love to hide himself and Jonty away here forever, beyond the cold, hard world they'd both come to know, but the needs of his little boy marched their way into his mind as they always did. "Apart from having to return for the court case, it's Jonty's home, where his therapist is."

He breathed deeply. *And where I'll face losing my son all over again.*

The tan skin of her cheeks blossomed in a smile, and his chest staggered at the beauty of the look she gave him. "I know you want an answer from me, Cy, but I still have a lot to consider. I'll let you know tomorrow."

She knew him so well, knew what made his heart beat harder, his body feel alive, and she understood that none of that mattered to him any more. Everything was for Jonty.

Her generous smile arrowed straight into his soul. "You make such a lovely dad."

4

"Is he *insane*? Are *you* for even giving this a second's consideration?" Fleur waved a spatula in the air and shook her head. "Has all that planning and number crunching for the renovation emptied your head of the working brain cells? How can you even be giving this head space?"

Ellie sat at the old kitchen table at Starfish Cottage later the next afternoon and continued to deflect her sister's outrage at what Cy had asked her to do. Fleur was rolling her eyes as she spoke, but Ellie could hear the concern in her voice.

"It's just plain rude. You can't be seriously considering it."

"I'm not going to say yes," Ellie said as she drew her finger up a line of frosting dribbling from the bowl in front of her. "But talking about it helps quiet that little voice inside that says I should at least think it through."

Fleur drew her lips together. "Sure you can *think* about it, and then you can tell him to sod off and not be so selfish." She placed a completed cupcake on a little plate. Delicate orange swirls danced around its edges. "I get that he's in a terrible situation, but how can he possibly expect you to give up your life, something you've worked so hard for, and to effectively break the law, when he hasn't seen you in years? And the last time he didn't even say goodbye."

Ellie licked her finger and let the sweetness fill her mouth. "Because he's out of options, and I'm the only one he can ask, the only one who knows him well enough. Imagine if you were in that situation."

"Have you talked to your life coaching girls about it?"

"Not yet, we're due for a call in half an hour, so I guess I'll tell them about it, but their reaction will be the same as yours."

Fleur wiped her hands on her apron, pulled out a chair, and sat down. "It is a horrible situation and I feel for that poor little boy, but this is Cy's problem, not yours, Ellie." Her tone became softer. "The only reason he's asked you to do this is because he knows what a kind heart you have. But he's taken your heart for granted once before and I'm not having him trample all over it again. If it was anyone else, it wouldn't be so bad, but Cy..."

Ellie reached out and touched her sister's slim wrist. Fleur knew she and Cy had slept together, that Ellie had told him she loved him and that he'd run. But not the rest of it. Through the years she'd been so tempted to unburden herself on Fleur, tell her what had really happened the day William died, but that seemed selfish now somehow. Nothing good could come from dragging all that up again. "No one's going to be trampling on anyone's heart," she said with a small smile.

"And how did he think it could work? Imagine being with him day in, day out for an entire year, touching him, pretending you're in *love*." Her eyes widened. "God, can you imagine looking at *that* body when it got out of the shower every morning and not being able to do anything with it? That could seriously screw with anyone's head."

Heat rushed to Ellie's cheeks, and she chuckled. She might have had that thought once or twice in the last few hours.

Fleur's voice dropped further. "Especially if you were still in love with him."

Ellie moistened her lips and stared at the cheery cupcake. "Well, I'm *not* going to marry him, so it's not an issue." She lifted her gaze to her sister again. "Besides, what makes you think I'd be in love when I haven't seen him in nearly a decade, anyway?"

Fleur stilled. "Maybe it's in the way you've still talked about him over the years, that faded photo of the two of you that's hiding on your bookcase." She tilted her head and narrowed her eyes. "Ellie, look me in the face and tell me you're not considering this."

Ellie just smiled. Of course, Fleur wasn't saying anything she hadn't thought herself in the hours she'd been turning Cy's proposal over in her mind. If she agreed, she'd have to pretend they were in love, have to touch him, be close. Maybe even share a bed together so people believed they were husband and wife. Oh, God, that was a new thought.

She shifted in her chair as her whole body hummed at the prospect of being that close to him. But there was so much else to consider, the fact that she had projects lined up for the next year, that being responsible for a child would require a skill set she just didn't have.

She twisted the plate in front of her. "I don't know how I can face him and say I'm not going to do the only thing that will help win his son back."

"Mmm hmmm." Fleur made the noise their mother always

made when she didn't really believe what someone was saying, and Ellie chuckled. "You don't think you're just hoping for a last little opportunity to have Cy jump your bones again? You're not secretly imagining you could turn him on to loving you in the time you were together? That would be a hell of a long time to be living so closely with someone as gorgeous as Cy."

Ellie shook her head. "No, he'd never love me. He's always made that clear, and he wouldn't have asked if he thought I still had feelings for him, would he? That would just be plain cruel."

"Seen my skim board?" Louis, Ellie's nine-year-old nephew, stood in the doorway in his boardshorts. He wore a baseball cap backward and flip-flops.

Fleur turned her head. "No, I haven't, sweetie. Hey, guess what? Ellie's invited our old friend Cy and his little boy, Jonty, over for Christmas dinner. Jonty's from the States. Won't that be fun?"

"Cool," Louis said. He moved to the counter and picked up a spoon with frosting on it, and raised his eyebrows at Fleur.

She winked at him, and he grinned as he slipped the spoon between his lips.

Ellie's breath froze in her chest. That slow look of unspoken love between mother and son, the little gestures of devotion that only came from spending a lifetime with someone. Would Cy lose that with Jonty if she said no?

"Can I make strawberry ice cream for Christmas dinner like Nana taught me?" Louis asked as he gave the spoon another giant lick.

"Sure." His mother chuckled. "We can do a practice run tomorrow. I wonder if we should have a more traditional Christmas dinner or do some New Zealand favorites."

Louis chewed his lip. "That boy. Does he know how to skim?"

Ellie shrugged. "I don't know, hon. I don't think he's been on the beach much, so maybe not. He's a bit shy, but perhaps you can teach him when he gets to know you better."

"Don't they have beaches in America?"

"They do, but he doesn't live near one." She reached over for the teapot and poured more in her cup and then Fleur's. "He found a pukeko chick yesterday. I'll take you over to have a look at it if you like. They're going to release it when its sore foot's better." What would the timid Jonty be like on Christmas day and on all the days to follow? If she said yes to Cy, the challenge of developing a relationship with his little boy would be enormous.

If she said yes? Her subconscious had blindsided her and her heart skipped double time. What was really holding her back? Being in the States for a year would be a big financial strain on her business and would mean her dream of having a permanent base in New Zealand would be put back years, but losing that dream was nothing compared to Cy losing his son. She blinked and put the brakes on her runaway brain.

Louis nodded. "Can we take him out back to see the glow-worms when it's dark?"

She passed the milk jug to Fleur. "I'm not sure, love. Jonty's never been here before and he might be tired from his big trip, but I'll ask his dad."

Louis stuck his bottom lip out. "We never have boys 'round here, 'cept for Grandad. It'd be cool to go to the glow-worms with him. Can you ask his dad?" He turned around. "I'm gonna look for my board in the shed."

Fleur sat back in her chair. "Your face could double as a movie screen you're so transparent, Ellie Jacobs."

Ellie blinked. "What on Earth do you mean?"

Her sister held her with a challenging stare. "I mean, I can tell you're seriously considering saying yes to Cy."

Ellie drew a circle in the confectioner's sugar on the table and blew out a soft breath. "How do you think Louis would react if I said yes? He's so used to having me around that he'd think it was strange if I got married and moved away."

Fleur pushed the plate of cupcakes toward Ellie, then took one herself. "Ell, he's nine; the only things he cares about are surfing and basketball. The minute he discovered Cy's a surfer, he'd be his friend for life. If you were to tell him you're going to live with Cy, he'd think it was 'primo.' But..." She paused. "I think you should stop considering how this will affect other people and think about yourself."

Ellie nodded. "And then there's Mum and Dad. They won't be back from Europe till mid-February. By that time, we'd be in Colorado. I'd have to tell them something."

Fleur moved her mouth from side to side. "That's a tough one. On one hand, Mum would totally believe you'd get into a relationship with Cy, but she'd be pretty disappointed if you got married and she wasn't there."

Ellie held her sister's gaze. "So you'd support me in this? If I talked things through with Cy and we found a way to make it work, you wouldn't try to stop me?"

Fleur reached out a hand and squeezed her fingers. "Of course I'd support you. I don't think I could do it, but I understand that it'd bring some closure to all you went through with Cy. And everyone in the world knows what a big heart you have." She smiled softly. "I just want you to promise me one thing."

Relieved that her sister understood why she was considering this, Ellie grinned back. "What's that?"

"Don't let Cy break your heart all over again."

As Ellie squeezed her sister's hand back, she told herself the exact same thing.

~

Kirin: *I can understand why you're considering it, but I'm gonna be the voice of reason here, Ellie. This is not only illegal, it could seriously mess with your head. It's a really big fat* **DON'T DO IT** *from me.*

Ellie had the laptop balanced on her knee as she swung in the old hammock chair that hung from the Starfish deck. Kirin and Gwin had been as shocked and incredulous as Fleur when she'd told them about Cy's proposal, but she knew they'd be honest with her about what they thought and it was what she needed right now.

Ellie: *I know on both counts. But I also know he wouldn't have asked me unless he was absolutely desperate...*

Kirin: *This could impact your professional credibility too...*

Ellie posted a sad face and swung a little harder in her chair. She could always count on Kirin to be brutally honest. Her friend had been through a terrible time in the last few years and was all about not letting people take advantage and putting yourself first. That she was now kicking those haters to the kerb and taking her life back was a source of pride for her and Gwin.

Gwin: *I'd normally agree with you, Kirin, but there's a little boy involved here. In fact, he's the driving force behind Cy needing to ask something so outrageous. My sister put a baby up for adoption seventeen years ago and she's always said the only good thing to come out of that was that she knows she fought to* *give her boy a better life. That's exactly what Cy is doing. It's going to impact both Cy and Jonty hugely if they're cut out of each other's lives.*

Ellie: *God, this is so hard. I agree with you both and maybe if I had more time to consider this I could come to an answer that I know is the right one, but Cy needs to know by Christmas.*

Kirin: *I just want to know why Cy thinks this is an okay thing to ask of you. To ask of anyone, really.*

Ellie chewed her lip as her fingers hovered above her keyboard and then she just let it all out.

Ellie: *Remember that time in Sapphire's life coaching course and she asked us to talk about a pivotal moment in our lives?*

Gwin: *I do. You didn't share in the whole class chat, but when it was just the three of us, you said it was when your brother drowned. I know Kirin and I were both a mess when you told us about that day.*

Ellie: *That day I was with Cy on his uncle's yacht, which was tied up to the jetty. We were supposed to be watching William, and we got distracted. I asked Cy to lie for me that day. To say that William had wandered off. Cy did lie for me and I think that's why he feels he can ask me to do this for him.*

Gwin: *Oh, man, that's an enormous burden to carry around.*

Ellie: *Not even my sister knows the whole truth. I kept trying to tell her, but there was so much grief in our house that I didn't want to add to it.*

Kirin: *They're hardly the same thing. One was a panicked plea from a teenager who was grief stricken. Cy's asking you to uproot your life and go with him to the other side of the world and when he's got what he needs from you, he's going to drop you like a...*

Ellie: *I know. You're completely right.*

Kirin: *He's also asking you to lie to those people who have stood by you, your family and your neighbors.*

Ellie: *Fleur would know the truth but I couldn't risk telling my parents, or Cy's mom. There would likely to be questions from U.S immigration service and I'd hate for any of them to have to lie.*

Gwin: *If you say no, you'll always wonder. Especially if he doesn't get custody. You'll wonder if you supported him when he really needed you, how things might have been different. We don't talk about my sister giving her son up for adoption, but I can tell my mom always wonders how our lives might have been different if she hadn't. Oh, Ellie, this is such a tough call. Kirin's right that you have to protect yourself, but I bet your heart is telling you what the right thing to do is.*

Ellie: *Honestly, my heart is telling me to do it, but I know you're right about all of those other things, Kirin.*

Kirin: *I didn't used to be a big believer in the heart—which is kinda funny since I've traded on the Cooking with Hart tagline most of my life, but since I've known Blake, I've really tapped into how I feel. I love your heart, Ellie, so much that I want to protect it, that's all.*

Ellie: *I know you do.*

Gwin: *What I want to know is, can you trust him? I don't mean, are you sure he's telling you the truth about everything, I mean, can you really trust that he would think about you and your needs? Would he want to protect you from any fallout from this?*

Ellie bit her lip. An eight-year-old image stamped itself on her brain. Of the moment she asked Cy to lie for her—to carry her secret for the rest of his life. He'd done it, despite desperately wanting to come clean for his own peace of mind.

Ellie: *100%*

Gwin: *Then I think you have your answer right there. You're not teenagers anymore. And he's not asking you because you're* *convenient or because he wants to trick anyone. I think he's so desperate to be with his son that, despite never intending to call in that favor, he really has no choice.*

Kirin: *If you decide this is what you want to do, I want to help too. I have a team of incredible lawyers that I've worked with over the last year that I'd love to recommend. Also, if you come back, we can meet for the very first time!*

Ellie: *You girls are just everything. I can't thank you enough for the support you've given me.*

Gwin: *We're here for it, Ellie. No matter whether things are going well or things are difficult, please keep talking to us.*

Kirin: *I just want to say that Cy is incredibly lucky to have a friend like you.*

Ellie: *And so am I to have friends like you.*

Ellie knocked on Cy's door the following morning and waited. It seemed odd to be so formal. In the old days she'd have just bowled right on in, calling his name with her snorkel set swinging from her fingertips. But odd didn't describe what she was about to do.

She'd lain awake most of the night, running through everything he'd told her, everything he'd asked of her, all the obstacles Fleur had reminded her of. The story of how Jonty's mom had died, how Cy had been prevented from seeing his son, broke her heart, but she had to know more. Thinking about how a sham marriage between her and Cy would affect people—their families, each other, and most of all Jonty, made her brain ache.

Fostering dogs, running meals on wheels, babysitting for friends, she couldn't stop doing things to help. But now she did it all with an eye on her own happiness, too. And she *was* happy now. Her life was full. She had great friends, a loving family, and the best job in the world. She was confident, strong, and in charge of her own dreams. But would all that change if she spent the next year living with Cy and his little boy?

"Hey." Cy smiled as he stood at his opened door, a plain white tee hugging his torso, his hair mussed. Aviator sunglasses were perched on his head and he was barefoot in boardshorts. Good God, he was gorgeous, just as he'd always been. If she agreed to his plan, she was going to have to look at him like this—have him within touching distance—for three hundred and sixty-five days, and the thought was torture.

"Do you have a minute?"

He looked back into the house and dropped his voice. "Jonty's watching cartoons on my laptop. Is it okay if we talk out here?"

"Sure."

He called back to Jonty that he'd be on the deck, then closed the door behind him. Padding down the steps, he looked so much more relaxed than he had yesterday.

"Great day." They sat at a picnic table, and she flicked sunglasses down onto her face, desperate to make this feel normal.

"Amazing." He tilted his head and looked out at the breaking waves. "Wish I could go out for a surf sometime, but I don't think I'll leave Jonty with anyone again. Yesterday didn't go so well."

She ran her tongue over dry lips. "I've seen your Uncle Pete on your old yacht. Maybe you could take it out sometime with Jonty."

He nodded, but she could tell small talk was the last thing on his mind.

"I've come to discuss your proposal."

He put his forearms on the table and leaned forward. "I was hoping you had. And before you say anything, I want you to know that no matter what you decide, it *won't* affect our friendship. Now that we're back in touch, I will not lose our connection again."

Their friendship. That precious thing that'd been destroyed by telling him she loved him and by him leaving without a backward glance. She couldn't do much more damage than that today. But once they'd had this conversation, their relationship would never be the same. She was sure of that.

"Cy, I want you to know that I've agonized over this. And the big question I have is, are you sure that marrying me is your only option?"

He scrubbed a hand across the stubble on his chin and nodded. "I've worked through every solution before getting to this point. I've tried to communicate with Susan's parents, tried to appeal to them on every level I could, but they'll only speak through lawyers. They've only agreed to me bringing Jonty back here for two weeks before the hearing, and that's only because they think it'll be too much for me and I'll give Jonty up." His Adam's apple jumped as he swallowed. "They couldn't be more wrong."

"Then how did you come up with the plan to marry me?"

His mouth lifted. "The minute I saw that letter from you, I remembered the friendship we'd had, what we'd been through together, and I knew it was something I could ask you to do."

She'd asked something pretty huge of him once, and now he was calling that favor in. He hooked her with those ocean-blue eyes and she couldn't look away, her heart clenching in her chest.

"I trust you, Ellie. Like no one else in my world, I trust you won't judge me, that you'll understand that I can't lose my son."

She played with a splinter of wood on the table as her stomach looped. "How would it work? I have this project to oversee, a restoration in Greece in March, but I'd need to be with you in the States. And I know nothing about children."

"That's right. We'd get married in Auckland before you came back with me. You'd only need to stay for a year at the most."

"How do you think it would affect Jonty? Wouldn't it create a whole new set of problems, having me come into his life and then leave again?"

He shrugged. "If you left after the year, I guess it would depend on how we dealt with it. Whenever you decided to come back, we'd still see you at the cove in the holidays, Christmas at least. The whole beauty of doing this with a friend means you can always be in our lives."

She chewed her lip. Of course, that was true. He'd only ever see her as a friend, nothing more. "And our families, what would we tell them?"

"No one can know the truth. For this to be one hundred percent watertight, we need *everyone* believing it's a genuine relationship, that what you and I have is a stable, committed marriage that will be the best environment for Jonty to be brought up in. Mum's still in her first job out of law school. She finished her study when she split from Dad. It wouldn't be fair to tell her something that could jeopardize her job if anyone found out that she'd known. How about your family?"

The thought of lying to her family again made bile sting

the back of the throat. "I've already mentioned it to Fleur. I had to tell her."

Slowly, he turned to face her more and nodded. "Okay, just Fleur." He was quiet for a second. "Does this mean you'll do it?"

She took a deep breath and her heart drummed deep in her chest. There wasn't a choice here. A little boy needed his dad, and she owed a good friend more than she could ever pay back. As long as she kept her heart safe, as long as he understood that she couldn't give him more than a year, then there was only one answer.

"I'll do it. For a year I'll be your wife, we'll live as if we're a happily married couple, and then we go our separate ways."

5

———

*C*y locked his hands tight on the tabletop to stop himself from reaching across and hugging Ellie. In the past, he would've done it without thinking, but now he wasn't sure how she'd react. She was so different from how she'd been in the past, so strong and confident—and still so beautiful—and he couldn't trust that his body wouldn't respond to her.

He didn't deny for a second that the next few months were going to be a crazy roller coaster, but this was his last chance to be with his son and he wasn't going to blow it.

She pushed a ringlet from her face and smiled. "So, what's the first thing we need to do?"

His shoulders relaxed. "We'll need to make wedding plans. I was thinking we could go to Auckland on the twenty-ninth to get the license and put everything in place, and then we could get married on the fourth or fifth before flying out."

She blew out a breath. "Wow, I guess we need to get things moving then."

"We have to make this as real as possible. The immigration and court authorities are going to be suspicious, so we need to make sure we have plenty of people who can vouch for our story."

She gave him an ironic smile. "I guess we've had some practice at telling lies." She played with a splinter on the table. "We established that I'm not in a relationship right now and I'm guessing there are no women in your life if you want me to come live with you."

She lifted her eyes, and he was pulled in by their softness.

"No, and there won't be. Jonty's my priority from now on. After everything my father put me through...Jonty deserves better. I'd like us to throw an engagement party. As soon as possible."

Something shifted on her face and her eyes widened. "Here? Now? But the authorities won't interview any of the people in the cove."

"We can't take the chance. If we say we've spent most of our relationship apart, that we've grown together through phoning and e-mailing, then there's going to be no one in the States who knows you. The sooner you and I act like a couple here, the better."

"But everyone in the hall yesterday saw you arrive. They didn't see us hug or kiss. And we're not staying in the same house. They wouldn't buy it."

He nodded. "I've been thinking about that. We can say that our relationship has grown via FaceTime over the last few months, that I decided to come back here so we could take it to the next level. We can explain away the meeting yesterday as me not wanting you to be involved in the project because it would keep us apart longer and then coming round when I saw everyone in the hall. We can say we've brought the wedding forward so we can be together sooner. And it's not weird we're in different houses when they're both so small and you're with Fleur and Louis."

"You certainly have it all worked out." Ellie sighed and rubbed her hands down her cheeks.

"What is it?"

"It all just sounds so complicated. I've lied enough in my life. I didn't want to have to do it again, especially not when it involved you. What if I forget the story?"

"You won't forget, and we don't have a choice. The only part of it we're really lying about is that we're in love. In every other way, isn't this something friends would do for each other?"

She put her fingers to her lips and hooked him with her stare. Her eyes were filled with honesty, such trusting honesty that his gut clenched. He'd never forget what she was doing for him, never forget her open heart and her sunny smile.

"Okay then, even though we've got so many details to work out, our stories to get straight, and plans to put in place, I'm willing to get on with showing the world we're a couple."

Unable to stop himself from touching her this time, he reached for her hands. "I knew you'd say yes, Ellie. Your generosity, your kindness...when I walked back into that hall again yesterday, I could see you were still the caring, giving person you've always been. Thank you. Thank you from the bottom of my heart."

~

The next afternoon, Cy walked out of Starfish Cottage carrying two cold beers in one hand, Jonty's hand tucked in the other. Along with the beer, they'd bought the last six bottles of sparkling wine at the tiny local store and had told Tom, the owner, they were celebrating their engagement.

It wasn't long before word got out and now people were arriving with drinks and plates of party food. The smell of barbecue and the tang of seaside air filled his lungs, and he breathed it deep.

Three days ago he couldn't have imagined feeling this positive, this pumped, about facing the custody battle back home, and the thought of sharing the next year with Ellie was the icing on the cake. She calmed him, centered him, and seeing the strength she'd gained in her life fired him on to find it for himself, too. He was grateful to have her back in his life. Maybe it could be permanent if things went well. A second chance had always been on his mind. Running from her was his single greatest regret.

He crouched down and pulled his son closer, and Jonty's warm body molded to his. "Shall we go say hi to Louis, the boy I told you about? I knew him when he was a tiny baby."

Ellie's nephew was sitting under a tree playing on his iPad. It had taken Cy all afternoon to get Jonty to come and meet Fleur and Louis. Gradually, he'd helped set up for the party, taking quick glances at the older boy out the corner of his eye. He'd watched Fleur string fairy lights in the pōhutukawa trees and then sat playing with paper napkins while Louis laid the two long tables and Cy prepared the barbecue.

They arrived at Louis's tree. "Hi, Jonty," the other boy said as he held out his iPad. "Wanna come look at what I've built on Minecraft?" Louis, patient and kind, just like his aunt, chatted to Jonty nonstop, as if there was nothing unusual about not receiving an answer.

"Hey, boys, there's some soda in the chiller if you want

some," he said. "And potato chips in the kitchen. I'll get them if you like."

"We can," Louis said as he stood and put his hand on Jonty's shoulder. "Let's go, J." Jonty looked up at his father and Cy nodded. He pulled in a breath. Louis waved his hand for Jonty to follow, and to Cy's amazement, he did.

He watched his son trot into the house after Ellie's nephew and his chest constricted. What must this all be like for him? A whole new country, new people, and now a whole new set of circumstances to deal with. Jonty making a friend in Louis was more than he'd hoped for.

Jonty knew the party was to celebrate the fact Ellie would be coming back to the States with them, but nothing more. There would be time to tell him about the marriage after he got to know her better.

Cy crossed to where Ellie was laughing with a couple of neighbors. The late afternoon sun threw sparkles on her hair and her face glowed. "Here you are, sweetheart." He handed her a beer, and when he moved in to kiss her on the cheek, she jerked back in reflex.

"Oh!" Her eyes were round, lips parted, and then her face suddenly changed. "Thanks, honey." She put the bottle on the table.

She leaned in, her lips cool as she pressed them into his cheek, but it was the scent of her that made his blood flow faster. A heady mixture of flowers and sunshine danced around him and he breathed her deep. She wore a tank top that hugged her breasts and a flowery skirt to her knees. Her hair was tied back in a loose ponytail and she wore gold hoops in her ears.

He hooked his hand around her waist and drew her close as the neighbors kept talking. And then his stomach muscles contracted as her hand moved to his back, the warmth of her touch penetrating through his T-shirt.

"Cy?"

"Sorry, I missed that." He tried to concentrate on what the guy in front of him was saying, while every cell seemed focused on where their bodies were connected.

"I was asking about your work."

He launched into a reply about what he loved about surfing and being on the retail side of it, but all the while, his body was firing to life with the feel of Ellie under his hand. His fingers relaxed on the curve of her hip, fitting together like two pieces of a puzzle.

"So, you had one of those online romances?"

Ellie turned to Cy, and he put his beer on the table and pulled her closer still. The thin strap on her shoulder slipped a little, and he hooked his fingers under it and drew it back up. Her skin was kissed golden and smooth and he couldn't help running his palm over it.

"You know what it's like, Ben." She laughed as her fingers circled her throat. "It's pretty easy to connect again these days."

"Facebook?" Ben's eyebrows rose.

"Was it Facebook, honey?" She dug her fingers into his side and he had to suppress a laugh. They'd have to do this repeatedly, the story of how they'd met and fallen in love.

"Twitter or Instagram or one of those things I think." He touched her cheek and light danced in her eyes. "All I know is that when we were back in touch, it was like we'd never been apart."

The laughter in her eyes suddenly changed, and a rose glow swept across her cheeks as she looked away. Her hand dropped from his waist and she reached for the beer. She lifted the bottle to her lips. Was she feeling this connection as much as he was, or was she just embarrassed by all the playacting?

"As long as you'll still let Ellie do the renovation here, we won't stop you," someone said.

"I love this place. Always have," he said. "And when I realized how much it meant to Ellie, how long she'd been working on it, there wasn't an option. She'll be seeing the project through, won't you, honey?"

Ellie rubbed a hand across her lips. "Cy wasn't sure he wanted us to be involved with the renovation, but when he saw so much interest in the hall yesterday and the fact people were so concerned, he knew it was the right thing to do." She dropped her hand, and he held her closer.

"Congratulations, you two!" Betty Browning joined the group and pushed a plate of club sandwiches into the middle of them. "I always knew you had something going for you. Everyone still remembers how sweet Ellie was on you, Cy, but the way you looked at her when you walked into the hall the other day, anyone could see you'd finally come to your senses."

Ellie's palm was warm against his and he squeezed her fingers as Betty passed the plate to the woman on her left and reached into her bag.

Betty continued. "A man doesn't look at a woman like that without there being some heavy-duty lusting going on."

Ellie squeezed his fingers back, and he saw the edges of her mouth tip up.

A few of the group chuckled, and Ellie turned to Cy again and looked into his face. She raised an eyebrow. "Lusting, is it?" She let go of his hand and trailed her fingers up his back until they rested on his shoulder.

He hadn't been aware of lusting after her in the hall, but

his body was doing a pretty good impression of feeling that way about her right now.

Betty nodded. "I've always said you can tell a man's intentions by the way his voice changes when he talks to his sweetheart, and that's exactly what happens with you, Cy."

He held Ellie's gaze. "Ellie would make any guy speechless, don't you think, Betty?" The tiny grin at the corner of Ellie's mouth slipped as she blinked and looked away. She *was* feeling something, too.

"And we haven't seen the ring!" Betty took her arm and Ellie dropped her hand from his hair.

A ring. He hadn't thought of that. They'd pick one out when they went to Auckland for the marriage license.

"We're getting married in Auckland after New Year's. In fact, we're going there on the twenty-ninth to make wedding arrangements, so maybe we'll get one then," Ellie said. "Cy needs to be back in the States for a few months and we'd prefer to get married here before we go. I'll be keeping a sharp eye on the council and the renovations from there, though."

Betty drew an ancient looking camera out of the navy-blue handbag on her wrist. "Now, I want a photo of you for my album. I have one of you both when you came to help me clear my front yard after a storm one year. It'd tickle my fancy to put a snap of you newly engaged beside it." She shooed the group to the side and took a step back.

Cy put his arm around Ellie's shoulder and she shuffled closer and turned, her soft breasts pressing into his side.

Betty beamed. "A kiss, please."

Ellie whispered under her breath, "Oh, no!"

He looked down into her face and whispered back. "I can make an excuse." He winked. "Or we could make the best of it."

"I've just put fresh lipstick on," she said to Betty in a helpless voice, and the older lady scoffed.

"What else is lipstick for than to be kissed off by a man as handsome as Cy?" She waved them together and lifted the camera to her eyes. "Hurry before the light changes."

He reached out and put his palms on Ellie's shoulders, his hands molding to the shape of her body.

She tilted her head to the side and the only sound was the screeching song of a cicada on the branch above them. For some inexplicable reason, he didn't want to get this wrong. His heart thumped, and blood tore through his veins.

Gently, he cupped her face in his hands. Her lips were plump and dusky, and a little moist from the remnants of beer. He leaned closer and her pupils dilated. He hoped she wanted to kiss him in that second, just as much as he wanted to lose himself in her.

Betty's shriek stopped them dead. "Oh, for the love of Michael! The batteries are dead! Do you have some I could borrow, Ellie?"

They both turned to her and Ellie stepped away, the warmth of her cheeks still imprinted on his fingertips. Ellie rearranged her tank top as a blush trailed across her face. "I'm sure there must be some in the house, Betty. I'll look for you later. Why don't I pass some nibbles around?"

"Thanks, but you'll still owe me that shot."

Betty turned to talk to the guy next to her and Cy tried to catch Ellie's eye. She wouldn't look at him. What had happened just then was so much more than make believe, and it threw a whole extra complication into their plan. He held back a groan. He'd have to keep a lid on it for now—no way would he give in to a rogue attraction and risk scaring Ellie off before he'd gained custody of his son.

"Oh, there you are." Fleur joined them, waving a pair of tongs in her hand. Ellie had told him that her sister knew about the marriage, and although he hadn't spoken to Fleur about it himself, he had the impression that she didn't think it was such a great idea.

"Won't your parents be proud of your sister, Fleur?" Betty said as she took a sandwich Ellie offered her. "What with losing your little brother and then you with Louis's no-good father running off, a wedding full of love will be just what they need. I bet your mum's shopping for an outfit on that overseas trip."

Fleur touched Cy on the back and threw him a teasing smile. "Oh, they'll be proud, all right. How could they not be happy with someone like Cy having Ellie's best interests at heart?"

Cy considered the elder Jacobs sister and raised an eyebrow at her challenge. "I'm the one who'll be proud," he said, meaning every word. "Having Ellie as my wife is a privilege I take seriously."

Fleur chewed the inside of her cheek and smiled back at him.

"Let's check on the barbecue," Ellie suddenly said as she took Cy's hand. "You take a break, Fleur. I think Betty wants to ask you for a cupcake recipe."

Before her sister replied, Ellie had him by the hand and was leading him to the secluded barbecue area. "Sorry about that," she whispered. "Fleur's a little overprotective."

"As she should be," he said, lowering his voice. "You're lucky to have such a strong family, Ellie. People to look out for you." He picked up a pair of tongs and started turning some kebabs. "How are you doing with all this?"

She sat on a swing hung in the tree and pushed her hair off her face. "To be honest, I'm not loving it. All the pretending. I can feel myself blush every time I have to lie."

He threw her a smile. "I wouldn't worry. People like Betty will think it's just your way of showing how in love with me you are."

She threw her head back and laughed. "I reckon we've got Betty fooled, and if she thinks we're in love, then half the province will know by tomorrow. Those drama classes Mum so reluctantly paid for one summer obviously paid off. I thought I must have been giving the game away for sure."

He sat his beer bottle on the side of the barbecue and waited until she looked at him. "No one can mistake the fact that we're still good friends. We'll just have to be ready next time someone expects us to act like a couple in love."

A wave of pink traveled up her neck. "I'm worried I'll forget and ruin everything."

"We'll be fine. We're comfortable enough around each other to pull it off."

She looked around to make sure no one was listening and her voice became more serious. "We'll need to discuss a few things like that. About boundaries."

He shrugged. "The best thing about being here for the next two weeks is that we can work on all that stuff. And the easiest way to get to know each other again is to spend time together, have some fun. It won't take us long to figure it out."

"Hey, speaking of having fun, Louis was asking if we could take Jonty to see the glow-worms down by the river. There's supposed to be a cold wind coming up tomorrow, so tonight would be good. I know it would mean a lot to Lou."

He turned sausages on the grill. "Louis's a great kid. It was nice of him to ask, but Jonty's scared of the dark. He still sleeps with a light on. I think it'd be too much."

"Even if we have torches and all go together? There's a good track down there now."

She didn't understand what it was like sometimes with Jonty. He could have a panic attack at any minute, either going still and refusing to move, or thrashing about so much that he could hurt himself. "I don't want to rush things with him, Ellie. With you coming back to the States now and the changes he'll have to go through living with us, he's going to have a lot to deal with. I'd prefer to play it safe."

"Sure," she said. "What do I know about kids, anyway? When Louis was three, I thought it would be a great idea to take him to see the fireworks at the neighbor's and it scared him witless."

"I'm sure you're great with kids," he said before taking another sip of beer. He saw the way she spoke to Louis, with love and devotion, and he only hoped he could help her build some sort of relationship with Jonty—and eventually him.

She nibbled her lip, then jumped off the swing and came to stand beside him. "It's great to have you back, Cy, really great, and I have a feeling that everything's going to turn out fine."

She turned away to pick up a bowl of corncobs and he watched the way the dusky light cast soft shadows on her face. It felt good to be back here, way more than he'd imagined, but it wasn't the relaxed lifestyle or the beautiful scenery that was getting under his skin. It was the beautiful Ellie Jacobs. He hoped that the connection to her he could feel growing every minute wouldn't cause everything to be blown apart.

∼

The night was still and black when they'd finished dinner and everyone else had gone home. The cool breeze had dropped, and the earth had come alive, heating from within as mosquitoes hummed and a morepork owl hooted in the distance.

Ellie watched Cy lean his forearms on the picnic table as he spoke. "That was great ice cream, Louis."

Louis looked down at the table and shrugged.

Cy scooped up the last bit of creamy residue with his finger before sliding it into his mouth. "Wish I could make ice cream. I can make a mean chocolate cake, but wouldn't know where to start with ice cream."

Louis's eyes flicked up, then down. "It's easy, but you've gotta use big eggs."

Cy nodded. "We've been doing eggs for breakfast since we got here, haven't we, Jonty? We like them with lots of ketchup."

Ellie made a gagging sound. "Ugh, you're kidding! That sounds nasty."

"No, it's not," Louis said. "It's what boys like, isn't it, Cy?"

"Sure is. Almost as good as chocolate sauce on pancakes for breakfast."

"I can do pancakes!" Louis's chin shot up. "I can do them with peanut butter, too, and my best ones have chocolate chunks."

Ellie and Fleur both poked their tongues out.

Cy winked across the table. "Maybe we'll have a boys' breakfast sometime. What do you say, Louis? Eggs and ketchup, chocolate chunk pancakes and a few sausages on the side. You can come to our place."

"Have you still got that pukeko chick?" Fleur asked.

Cy nodded. "Ellie called the bird sanctuary, and they said not to release it until its foot was better. They can take it after the Christmas break to get it ready to go back into the wild. Jonty's been looking after it really well, haven't you, bud?"

Jonty dragged the spoon through his lips and nodded to his father. He played with the scarf that was always tied around his neck or wrist.

Louis pushed his chair back. "Can we see the glow-worms?"

Ellie shot a look at Cy. "I forgot to tell him."

"I think Jonty's a bit tired tonight, aren't you, J?" Cy said

Jonty's eyes widened, and he shook his head vigorously.

Cy swiveled toward his son. "There are no lights where the glow-worms are. You can only see them when it's really dark at night. In the forest."

Sensing a moment of tension, Ellie said, "You'll be here for lots of nights, Jonty. We can see the glow-worms another time. Has Daddy told you about them?" Cy's little boy just looked at her and she rushed on, cursing herself for asking a question he couldn't answer. "They're a bit like lightening bugs, but they're worms that live on the banks of the stream. You can only see them at night. When you're really, really quiet and everything's really dark, they shine brightly, like the fairy lights you helped Fleur put in the trees."

Jonty put his spoon on the plate and as he looked at her, blinking, Ellie's heart did a swan dive. Connecting with him was going to be so hard. And reconnecting with his dad was going to be even harder.

Jonty turned to Louis.

"Pleeeease," Louis said to Cy. "Tell him, Ellie. It'll be great. Jonty's never seen them before and I want to show him. Please!"

Fleur stood and lifted a jacket from the back of a chair. "If we're going, it needs to be soon. I don't want you too tired for Christmas prep tomorrow, Louis." Cy stayed seated at the table and Ellie could see how torn he was. It must be tough to balance trying to protect his son with the fact Jonty seemed so keen to go. Perhaps if Cy could relax a little, then Jonty would relax too.

~

The weight of their stares caused Cy to sigh. "All right, but you'll need to hold my hand all the way. He stood and put Jonty's jacket on while Louis whooped around, looking for torches.

While he bundled his boy up, Cy wondered what had made him agree to take Jonty to the glow-worms. It could've been the desperation in Louis's voice, might also have been the brightness in Jonty's eyes, but if he were honest with himself, the real reason was that he didn't want this day with Ellie to end.

So much of the afternoon at the party had been about pretending and playacting, but when the visitors had gone and they could get back to being themselves, everything felt so different. They'd laughed together again and talked about the things Ellie would find different in the States. When they'd sat down to dinner together under the lights in the old rata tree, Cy had realized that he hadn't felt this connected to anyone in years, and he didn't want it to stop.

A short while later, they were walking through the bush, the scent of overripe summer flowers surrounding them. Cy held Jonty's hand beside Ellie, with Fleur and Louis taking the lead. Fleur was telling them all an old Māori legend about the fairy people who'd visit the river as glow-worms, Louis embellishing it with hoots and whoops.

Cy shared a flashlight with Ellie and stayed close to her

in the darkness. His heavy footfalls on dried ferns beat time. "Remember when my old friend Jake and I followed a bunch of you girls down here one night and pretended to be ghosts?" He looked down to check for roots in their way and saw Ellie smile in the flashlight's glow.

She laughed. "We screamed so much, all the dads came running and two of them ended up in the river."

He chuckled. "We got in big trouble."

"And your punishment was to help clean out the septic tanks."

Cy let the memory of those simple times wash through him. So much had happened since.

"Hey, J," Louis called. "There's a possum in the tree up here. Come take a look."

Jonty pulled away, but Cy still held his hand. "Will you be okay?"

Jonty turned to look at Ellie.

"I'm sure he'll be fine, won't you, Jonty," she said quietly.

Jonty nodded and slipped from Cy's hold. Ellie stopped and hugged herself at his side.

"You're cold," he said and stopped walking.

She pulled her cardigan tighter. "I'm okay."

He ignored her protest and shrugged out of his jacket, the light from the flashlight casting soft shadows across her face. Ahead, Jonty moved his flashlight this way and that as they looked for the possum.

Cy held the jacket behind her and Ellie put her arms through the holes till her fingers were swamped. When he'd adjusted it, he held his hands on her shoulders for a moment and his stomach looped. He turned her around, and she rolled the sleeve so she could hold the flashlight better.

"This zipper's a bit funny. I'll do it up for you," he said.

He drew the bottom edges of the jacket together as she watched.

When he reached her chest, his mind flashed to that day on the yacht years ago, how her body responded to him. The memory caused his chest to tighten. His responses had been naïve then, rapid and reflex. The way his body awakened now was from knowledge of the way he wanted to make her feel.

He held his breath as he reached her heart. For a second he fumbled, but still Ellie didn't look up, and he was afraid that the spell he was under would be broken. Not wanting to finish his task, he rested his hands on her shoulders and Ellie's gaze drifted up. She stood still, night shadows dancing across her face. Did she feel what he did? His heart squeezed as he reached down and took her hand in his. "Better?"

"Mm hmm," she murmured.

Then he looked over her shoulder. "Wait up, you guys," he called, while he ordered his heart to slow and his body to regain its equilibrium.

What had just happened? Had he imagined the thread of electricity dancing between them? Was the spark that had begun a slow-burning fire in his blood nothing more than wishful thinking?

"Shh! We're here," Louis called from up ahead.

Cy could make out shapes stopped on the track and gave a vote of thanks for the distraction. He stopped alongside Jonty and put a hand on his son's shoulder and drew the boy to him.

"Okay, everyone, on the count of three," Fleur whispered. "Turn off your flashlights and look across to the banks of the stream. Don't make any noise or their lights will go out."

Cy reached for his son's hand and held it warm in his own.

"One, two, three."

As they were plunged into darkness, Jonty breathed in sharply and squeezed his hand before burying his face in Cy's thigh.

Cy knelt. "It's okay, J." And he took in a swift breath of his own as the sight in front of them came into sharp focus. "Look, Jonty, look." Still, the little boy's face was squashed into his leg as Cy turned and stared at the millions of tiny lights twinkling like diamonds.

"Wow, Jonty. Isn't it cool?" Louis whispered.

Jonty's hands moved to his face, and he slapped his palms over his eyes and rocked backward and forward. Cold, piercing fear gripped Cy as he reached for his son's shoulders and pulled him close. "Cy, is he okay?" Ellie was beside him in a second, her voice soft and full of concern.

Cy turned to face her. "No, he's not okay. He's scared of the dark and I shouldn't have brought him here." He scooped up Jonty, turned the flashlight back on, and pointed it up the track. Jonty was stiff in his arms, hands still stuck to his eyes.

"Cy, I'm sorry, I didn't..."

Cy rubbed his son's small, warm body. What the hell had he been thinking? He'd let himself be talked into something because of what *he* wanted, not what was best for his son. Jonty's needs were his priority, not his own physical desires.

Aside from that, if Ellie were to change her mind about marrying him because he couldn't keep focused on what was important, then he'd never forgive himself. That he'd lost sight of that made him curse quietly under his breath.

Starting tomorrow, there would be no more touching, no more being tempted. From now on, he'd be the gentleman he should've been all those years ago. He should have grown up in eight years—God knew he'd had plenty of reason to—and now was the time to act like it.

No matter how much his body and heart told him otherwise.

6

The twenty-third had dawned cool and gray, and Ellie pulled a cardigan around her shoulders as she carried the milk up the beach from the store. New Zealand in December...it could be searing hot one minute and freezing the next. Everything today—the sand, sea, sky —was silver. Even the sound of the wind in the enormous macrocarpa trees was sharp and metallic.

Her heart felt metallic too after last night. Why had she encouraged Jonty to go see the glow-worms when Cy had told her he'd be frightened? She was going to be partially responsible for that little boy for the next year, and the thought wasn't getting any easier. Being around children scared her. She didn't know how Fleur coped when Louis scraped his knees or came home crying because someone had been mean to him at school. What if she made things worse with Jonty's mutism rather than better?

She'd see Cy later. She'd apologize for pushing the glow worm visit and hope that they were still planning on coming for Christmas.

There were a hundred and one things to do in the next

two days. Wrap presents, try to make the mock Christmas tree made from driftwood and seaweed stay upright. And through all that, she'd try to stop thinking about the near-miss kiss with Cy at the barbecue. She'd replayed the moment their lips had almost touched over and over and the fantasy had grown from a fake attempt at a barbecue to a kiss in a bedroom, to a kiss while tangled in her sheets...

Before she reached the house, Louis shot down the stairs and out the gate.

"Louis," she called. "Where are you going?" She walked faster. He had a towel tied around his neck like a cape and something colorful under each arm. He held them high.

"Going to Jonty's," he called out. "Flying kites and boogie boarding. Mum's gone to town."

Fleur had left to go into Papaatawhai, the neighboring town, for last-minute Christmas supplies, and Ellie was supposed to be looking after her nephew. He was a great kid, but had the uncanny ability of sneaking off when she wasn't watching.

"Why the backpack?" she asked when she finally caught up to him, breath short. Faded jeans trailed from the top and a snorkel stuck out at an angle.

"Cy said he'd take us out on the yacht to Aroha Island if it was windy. We're gonna fly kites and maybe snorkel and catch some waves." He kept walking as he called over his shoulder.

"When did you organize this?" She struggled to keep up in the soft sand.

He shrugged. "Last night, before dinner. He said we could do it on the next windy day. Mum said it was okay and Cy said to ask you and Mum if you wanted to come, too."

Her heart dropped. "Honey, I don't think...I mean, after

the scare Jonty had last night, I'm not sure Cy will want to take him out on the yacht now."

"I went to their place this morning to check we were still going and Cy said we could."

Surprised, she looked down the beach and saw Cy and Jonty stepping out of their house. Cy looked up and waved, and she held up her hand as her chest tightened.

What would she say about what had happened with Jonty? "I can't come, sorry," she said. "I've got all sorts of things to get ready for tomorrow." She paused, trying to marshal her thoughts. "Did you ask your mum?"

He shrugged. "She was cool."

Ellie rolled her lip through her teeth, indecision cutting deep. She was certain Cy would be careful, but maybe it was too much to look after two children and sail a yacht?

Looking out at the waves, she let out a long breath. She was being ridiculous. Louis would be fine. And if Fleur had agreed to it last night, who was she to argue?

"Okay, you can go, Lou. Have a great time." She moved toward the Starfish gate as Cy and Jonty walked toward her.

"Hey," Cy said, throwing her a skin-tingling grin. A deep blue rash guard pulled tight across his chest and cut off cargos fringed at his tanned knees. The aviator glasses sat across his face, hiding his eyes. "Coming sailing? Pete's been maintaining the yacht, like you said. I had a look at her yesterday, and I think she's in better condition than when I left."

She concentrated on his face, looking for a sign that he was upset about last night. He looked exactly the same as he always did. Cool and sure. And handsome.

"I'm really sorry about last night," she said, dropping her voice as she turned to look at Jonty. "Is he okay?"

Cy ruffled his son's hair. "I should be the one apologizing. I shouldn't have reacted like that."

"Perhaps not. But I shouldn't have tried to convince you to go to the glow-worms, either."

"It was a timely reminder that Jonty can't be pushed too hard, but it was my decision to make, so the fault's mine."

"It's okay. It can be scary in the dark."

Jonty had his face turned to Louis.

Cy spoke to her, but obviously his words were for his son, too. "I talked to Jonty about what happened last night, and I said that what made me most proud was that he gave it a go. He was more ready than I was to try something new, so my motto for the next few weeks is giving things a go, including taking the boys out on the yacht, like I promised. Want to come?"

"Um, no thanks." She dragged sunglasses from her head to her face. "I've got too much to do today. You have fun, though." She cast a look at the choppy waves. "It's pretty windy out there."

"We'll have to wait until your mum gets back, Louis. We need two adults on the yacht." Cy laid his hand on the boy's shoulder. "We can go another time."

Louis scuffed his toe in the sand. "No point waiting for Mum," he said with a scowl. "She gets seasick in the tub."

All three male faces turned to Ellie and her heart fell. Somewhere inside, her body remembered the gentle sway as she'd stood on the yacht's deck, the way the teak beneath her feet warmed her whole body, but after the last time on Cy's yacht...

"What about the pukeko? Doesn't someone need to stay and look after him?" she said.

"We've built a makeshift coop," Cy said, "so it can run on grass instead of getting sore feet in the box."

She could hardly say she didn't know how to sail. Cy knew she could handle a boat as well as he could. But she needed a little more time away from him to get her fantasies under control. If she risked being in close quarters before she had that locked down, she might do something irrevocable, like kiss him for real.

"The turkey!" she said. "The pavlova and shelling the peas. Who'll get all that ready if I go sailing? We'll end up eating cereal for Christmas dinner."

"It's early," Cy said, throwing her a grin. "We can be back by lunchtime. It'd be nice to have you with us."

Ellie looked down at Jonty. The little boy's face was impassive as usual, but for some reason, she couldn't look away.

And couldn't say no.

"All right," she said, giving Cy a reluctant grin. "But I need to be back by lunchtime if we want to have any Christmas, okay?"

Cy clapped his hand on Louis's shoulder. "Excellent."

Half an hour later, they were near the jetty where Cy's uncle would bring the yacht from its mooring. Louis and Jonty explored the beach, while Ellie and Cy brought the last of the gear down from the car. When everything was waiting in a huge pile, Ellie kicked her flip-flops off, dug her toes into the cool sand, and looked out to sea.

"It's been so long since I've been to the island." She took off her sunglasses so she could see everything more clearly and put them on the ground, too. The wind had dropped and there was a gentle breeze. The boys were hunting through piles of driftwood at the high tide line. She kicked at the dry sand. "I wonder if that old shipwreck's still visible off the north side."

"I can't wait to get out there." Cy was standing, hands on hips, looking out to sea.

The day stretched in front of them. Relief that there was no lasting damage after last night and the thought that she'd be spending the morning with her oldest friend fizzed through Ellie's blood. In an unexplainable surge of energy, she threw her hands down on the sand and kicked her legs up in the air in a handstand. But her balance was all wrong, and she ended up falling in a heap on the sand, laughing.

"What in the hell was that?" Cy stood with his hands low on his hips. "You were about the best at handstands I've ever seen. What happened?"

She picked herself off the sand and stood up. "I got old, that's what happened. And my center of gravity's probably shifted from all the cream puffs I've eaten in the last eight years."

She looked up to see Louis and Jonty having a sword fight with two pieces of driftwood, then focused on another spot on the sand, determined to get it right this time. She launched herself forward, flicked her legs in the air, and after wobbling for a few seconds, fell with a *thud*.

Getting up again, she tugged her shorts from where they'd ridden up her legs, then smoothed the hair off her face. "I can't believe it! Must be you that's putting me off. Turn around."

"No way am I turning around," Cy said, his head tilted to one side and a sexy grin on his face. He pushed his sunglasses up. "This is worth paying good money for. I think you've lost your touch."

She chuckled and dusted the sand from her shorts. "I have not! Come here and make yourself useful. I might be out of practice, but I've still got it. I reckon I could stay up for at least a minute if you help steady me."

He took a step closer.

"Remember the drill? When I've flicked my legs up, just get me balanced and then I can do the rest on my own."

"Okay, if you're sure."

"I'm sure. Ready?"

"On the count of three. One...two...three..." This time when she threw herself forward and kicked her legs high into the air, Cy was ready to catch her, his palms warm and firm on her ankles as he held her steady. As soon as she could feel her center of gravity shifting, she yelled, "Okay, you can let go now."

And when he let go, she was balanced in a perfect line. Looking back, she could only see his muscular legs with a dusting of hair and then the fringed edge of his cargo cutoffs. Her hair was hot against her face, but she was determined to make it to sixty seconds.

"Bet you can't stay there very long," he teased.

"Are you watching the boys?" She took a couple of steps with her hands to balance.

"They're fine." He twisted a little. "They're still playing with the driftwood. Hey, that's pretty good going. Reckon you can do fifteen more seconds?"

Blood was pumping at her temples. As she adjusted one hand, her T-shirt started to ride down. In only a matter of seconds, her bra would be exposed, but their old competitiveness—the need to prove she could make the minute—outweighed modesty.

"Ten more seconds," Cy called. "Are you getting dizzy? Your T-shirt's slipping. You won't be able to see anything soon. And wow, is that red lace?"

Determined to stay the distance, Ellie panted. Her T-shirt was now over her face and she was overbalancing with her hands.

"Four, three, two…!"

"You rat!"

"One!"

She collapsed on the sand and gulped in fat lungful's of air.

Cy took a step toward her and held out a hand. "I take it all back," he said with a heart-stopping grin. "You've still got it."

Her breath was heavy in her chest and the air stilled around them as she looked up at Cy's broad palm. She reached out, and when her hand was enclosed in his sure grip, he gently pulled her to her feet. But she didn't pull back, didn't step away, instead she felt herself falling under his spell, imagining the touch and taste of his mouth on hers.

She flicked her gaze away, determined not to succumb, to resist touching those strong shoulders, that broad chest, because she knew if she did there'd be no going back.

Cy reached out with his other hand to cradle her cheek, and when he stepped closer, her heart raced. Slowly, she turned to look up at him as he cupped her whole face with both his hands and whispered, "Just go with it." Then his lips were pressed against hers, his breath feathering across her face, and she wound her hands around his neck.

With her blood fizzing everywhere Cy touched, her lips succumbing as he teased them with his tongue, she knew for sure that the connection she'd felt with Cy last night hadn't been imagined. When he lifted his mouth from hers and pulled her into a hug, she could feel his speeding heart against hers and she drew in a breath.

"Hey, you two," Cy said to someone behind them.

Ellie twisted around.

"Don't stop on our account." It was Callum Brown, Cy's old surfing buddy, and his wife, hand in hand with a small brown dog on a leash. They'd obviously been walking up the beach and Cy must have seen them before Ellie did. *Just go with it.* That was the reason he'd kissed her.

"Hey, Callum; hey, Lyn." Ellie hoped no one else noticed how fast she was speaking or that her breath was tight in her lungs. She slid her arm around Cy's back and pulled him closer, determined he wouldn't sense what a fool she'd just made of herself. "Sorry about the PDA!"

Lyn laughed and flicked her hair over her shoulder. "We had a little make out session on the beach a little while ago too, didn't we, hon?" She stroked her husband's arm. "Something about this sort of weather that makes all those hormones race, right?"

"Yeah, weather seems to be what does it for me." Cy chuckled. "Rain, sun, typhoon. Any weather, I'm not fussy."

They all laughed, then made small talk about what they were doing for Christmas and how great the fishing was off Aroha Island. When Lyn and Callum said goodbye and carried on with their walk, Cy turned to Ellie. "Hey, I'm sorry about that. I saw them coming toward us and thought it was a good opportunity to show a bit of spontaneous love. I hope I didn't take you by surprise?"

"Surprise?" She bent down to brush sand off her flip-flops, anything to avoid looking into his eyes. "No, of course not. I saw them coming, too, which was why I held your hand so long." She stood and smiled up at him. "I think we had them convinced."

He grinned back, and the relief on his face was like a kick to her gut. "I think we did, too." He called over her shoulder,

"Hey, boys, look. Here comes the boat." The boys raced over and Cy walked with them to the jetty as Ellie got angry with herself. How could she have been so stupid to think that was real? Just like last night, Cy was making a public show of their lie and she'd let her body be fooled into believing his reactions to her were real. Well, they weren't real, and never would be, and she was going to have to make her heart believe that.

In no time, they were on the yacht, heading straight for Aroha Island. The hard decking dug into Ellie's thighs and she tugged her shorts lower.

The boys were up front, hair blowing back, suited in their lifejackets and looking like two little sumo wrestlers. Jonty's scarf was wrapped around his neck and flapped in the wind. They were heading straight for Aroha Island and at this rate would be there in no time.

"Can you hold this for me, Ellie?" Cy passed her a metal shackle on the end of a rope. "Stand here while I hook it up." He reached closer and the fresh smell of him invaded her senses.

His chest was only inches from her face, muscles firm beneath. Between his proximity, the memory of the barbecue last night, and their connection back on the beach, her thoughts drifted to the last time she'd been on this boat. He hadn't known she was a virgin when they made love. Well, if he had, he'd never said. And that her very first time was overshadowed by the devastation of William's death, then the anguish of Cy's rejection when she told him she loved him, made it something she shouldn't want to remember. She shouldn't be drawn to the strength in his legs, the power in his shoulders, or wonder what it would be like to make love to him again.

"Ellie?"

She shook her head to clear the fantasy from her mind and looked up at him. "Sorry?"

He grinned. "I said you can let go now. Has the blood not made its way back to your body since the handstand? You look flustered."

Fire rushed to her cheeks as she let the clasp go. She stood back as he brushed his hands on his shorts and pulled the sunglasses from his face. "God, it feels good doing this again. I haven't even been for a surf since I got back." His smile stretched across his face. "Stand back, Jonty," he said and the little boy twisted to look at him, took a step back, then resumed his vigil.

He slung the glasses on the neck of his top and his lowered voice brimmed with enthusiasm. "I meant what I said before, about being overprotective. I know Jonty needs to experience things without me hovering over him. He looks pretty relaxed up there with Louis."

Ellie smiled as she watched Louis point out a gannet flying by.

"I've told him I'll try to get a paua shell today. He sits on the steps of the cottage and stares at the shells laid in the concrete. Dad left an old grinder in the shed, so I can shine it up for him."

Ellie lifted her face to the breeze, hair flying out behind her. "You're such a natural dad."

His stare heated her face. "Thank you. That means more than you know."

The rhythm of the boat caused her eyes to drift closed. "I think you're born to it. Being a parent. I must've missed that gene somehow. It won't happen for me."

"You're not going to have children?"

She opened her eyes but avoided his stare and sat on one of the fishing chairs. "No."

As he took the chair beside her, she finally looked at him. His jaw slackened as he scanned her face. "Ellie, you can't be serious."

The air stilled in her chest. She reached over to grab her bag, anything to avoid looking into his face. "Do you think we get cell coverage out here? I'm expecting a call from the council about some new plans."

His silence made her turn.

"What?"

He pinned her with his gaze. "You don't mean that. About not having children."

Tensing, she kept her voice calm. "Yes, I do."

"But why?"

Her skin cooled. She'd had this conversation with her mum, with Fleur, and people never really understood. Always wanted a reason. "I don't think I'm suited to it. Some people aren't. And my job means I need to travel and live all over the world. A baby doesn't fit into that."

He dropped his head and shook it, and the sun glinted off his dark blonde waves. "Not buying it."

She swallowed. "What do you mean, 'not buying it'?"

He looked up, and a dimple dug into his cheek. "I know you, Ellie. You're not the type of woman to walk away from being a mother. You've got too much love to give."

Her heart gave an extra beat. He didn't know her. Certainly not as a woman. And the only reason he'd said that was because she was about to be a temporary mother to his son.

"There's something more to it. Why don't you want to have children?"

She looked out to sea and concentrated on the rows of whitecaps dancing their way toward the yacht. "I've found something I'm good at in my life and it's going to take me all over the world. Being a mother's not a priority for me and I don't enjoy doing something unless I'm one hundred percent committed."

He said nothing, but she knew he wanted to, knew he'd have opinions.

"I've been lucky to be in Louis's life since he was born and that's enough for me." She brushed a sand fly from her arm.

"I wouldn't have picked it." He huffed a breath. "Wouldn't have picked it at all."

"People don't always stay the same, Cy." She smiled. "I'm not the same girl I was all those years ago."

He nodded and held her gaze for such a long moment that she squirmed. Had he considered siblings for Jonty? He'd said there was no room for another relationship in his life, but that would mean no brothers or sisters for his son. The sudden thought that this might be a part of his plan further down the track sent a chill across her skin. She was glad she'd said it now, glad he'd understand that wasn't something she could give him as well.

"Come on," he said. "We need to get the snorkeling gear ready."

"Snorkeling gear?" Her heart rate spiked.

He looked down at her, the aviator glasses and tight top making him look like a swimwear model. "I want to get Jonty's shell, and I told Louis I'd take him around the rocks."

Her tongue froze over the word. "Diving!"

"Just snorkeling." He moved to the side of the boat. "We won't go far, or for long, but he said he'd never been on the rocks around the island and I'd like to show him."

The fine hairs on her arm stood to attention. She was responsible for Louis. Could he swim well enough? A snake of fear wriggled up her back. Did Cy understand what he was doing? She fruitlessly checked her phone again for a signal. Perhaps if she could talk it through with Fleur, confirm that Cy had her sister's permission, she'd feel better...

The scrape of the anchor being let down jolted her from her thoughts.

"It's snorkeling, but we still need to make sure we stay warm. See, Jonty? Come and feel the fabric of the wetsuit. Feel how thick it is."

The two boys were watching Cy, so Ellie lowered her voice. "I'm not comfortable with this." She swallowed past the steel band tightening around her throat. He must know that this would bring back thoughts of William and the way he'd died.

"I asked Fleur, and she said it'd be fine. Louis is on his swim team at school, aren't you, son?"

Louis nodded vigorously.

"And he's done some snorkeling with Fleur." Cy's voice was low and calm.

Beat by beat, Ellie's pulse slowed. She was being silly. Of course he'd take care of Louis. She'd been around those rocks many times herself, and it really was beautiful.

"And I'm getting the shell for Jonty."

Ellie's brain stalled. "Jonty and I'll be waiting on the boat for you?" She'd be alone with Jonty. Responsible for him. Just as she was going to be when she was Cy's pretend wife and the thought chilled her.

Cy looked over to where his son was examining some ropes and lowered his voice. "I called Dr. Marlowe last night about the way Jonty reacted and he suggested I try some new strategies."

Ellie's head spun. "Strategies?"

Cy dug around in a large carry bag and dragged out

snorkels and fins. "Make more opportunities for Jonty to interact with other people. Be close enough so he can see me or even feel me, but so he knows he can cope on his own."

"So that's why you brought him sailing?"

"When he showed so much interest in the paua shells, I thought bringing him here was the perfect opportunity. Dr. Marlowe said that as long as Jonty takes an active part in deciding what he's comfortable with and what he's not, it should be positive. I told Jonty what we'd be doing today and I'm happy that he's comfortable with it. Unless you'd rather I drop you off on shore, but it'd be better if you can keep an eye on us from the deck."

What if he cried, or screamed for his father? Or what if he sat silently and stared at her and she didn't know what to do? What Cy wanted to do for his son was beautiful, but... She hadn't thought all this through before she'd said yes to the marriage. He hadn't mentioned it to her either, as if he just expected she'd be okay at this.

She was anything but.

Her lips froze, and she couldn't think of an answer.

Louis grabbed his own wetsuit and in minutes they were ready with masks on, flippers thumping on the deck.

Her fingers knotted together. "How long will you be?"

"Fifteen minutes at most." Cy knelt in front of his son. "You'll be fine, won't you, J? I'm going down to get one of those sparkly shells for you. Ellie will be right here. And remember, I told you she knows all sorts of things about the ocean."

Jonty stared at his father with enormous, unblinking eyes.

"And look." Cy's voice was quiet, gentle. "I've got this special rope that you get to hold." He clipped one end of a rope to a carabiner on his wetsuit and gave the other to Jonty. "You'll be holding on to me the whole time."

Jonty held the rope in his fat little fist and Ellie had to look away as her vision became clouded at what Cy was doing for his son.

Cy stood, his tall frame blocking the sun as he took a step toward her. "Will you be okay?" he asked. "I can take you to shore if you'd rather."

No. God, no. It would be bad enough being in charge of a six-year-old, let alone taking care of him on a beach.

"Will you be okay?" Cy repeated.

"I'm not worried about me," Ellie lied. "How will Jonty feel?"

"He'll be fine. We've talked a lot about me going into the water when I'm surfing and if he can hold on to the rope, he said he'll be okay."

Ellie steeled herself. She could do this. For half an hour, she could sit on a boat with a little boy and they could watch the seagulls dive into the ocean and it would be fine.

Minutes later, she sat beside Jonty on the deck of the yacht as he held the rope in his small fist and watched the spot where Louis and Cy were snorkeling. The cloud cover had lifted, and the sun burned down.

He'd had no reaction when his dad had gone over the side of the boat, except to lift the scarf so it covered his chin, close enough that it touched his lips if he wanted it to.

Ellie crossed her ankles and took a sip of the juice she'd poured for both of them. "It's getting hotter." She held the cool cup to her cheek. "How much sunscreen did Daddy put on you?"

She could've kicked herself. Open questions to Jonty were pointless. If she couldn't ask questions, what could she say?

A vision came floating into her mind of a time when her cousin Tim had pushed her off her bed and she'd had to get stitches. The memory of the fear and confusion was still very real. Maybe Jonty felt like that right now. Out of his depth, scared. Her heart melted.

She had to try something different. "There's not much I can remember about being six."

Jonty's gaze remained fixed on the water.

She stretched her legs and waggled her toes. "But there's one thing I *do* remember."

He pulled the scarf right over his lips. Maybe she was scaring him? God, this was hard.

"I can remember what made me feel better."

His eyes shot toward her, then away.

"I had a purple stuffed rabbit." She cleared her throat. "Called Mr. Tippity." She sent up a silent prayer that she wasn't making things worse. "He only had one ear 'cause I chewed the other one off when I got scared."

Jonty shifted on the decking.

"I think your scarf stops you from being scared and I wish I could have Mr. Tippity right now 'cause I'm a bit scared."

His gaze locked onto hers, and she smiled.

"I'm scared about Louis being under the water, but I know he's a good swimmer and that your dad will take really good care of him."

Jonty stroked the rope between his fingers. The only sound was the water slapping against the side of the yacht and the *clunk* as parts of the sail hit the mast.

"It was lovely of your dad to give you a scarf to stop you from being scared."

A shadow drew across his face, and Jonty slowly shook his head.

Ellie swallowed as her heart thumped. This was the first time he'd really acknowledged her, communicated, and her chest constricted.

She spoke over the ache within. "Your dad didn't give you the scarf?"

He kept on shaking his head and Ellie drew in a breath as she realized what he was saying.

"Your mum?" Her voice quavered. "That was your mummy's scarf, wasn't it?" And she held her breath as she waited for this beautiful boy to answer her with his eyes.

7

_____

Jonty held his head rigid, then with the slightest dip of his chin, nodded. As his eyes grew wider, a rush of blood pumped through Ellie's body. It might be without words, might be little more than a movement, but Jonty was communicating. This little boy who'd have to work out every day who and what to trust was answering her question. Tears pricked sharp behind her nose, but she forced them back.

He cast his gaze downward and slowly stopped moving. A black hole sucked her in and she struggled with what to say next. Children were so fragile, so easily influenced by the adults around them, and she prayed she didn't screw this up.

She knew what it was like to have someone erased from your life—the sense of complete bewilderment, the emptiness that deepened and decayed inside. And the well-meaning people around you who'd poke and prod for a reaction.

"Oh, it's beautiful," she said as she focused on his scarf. "Those are such great colors. I think they were probably

96

some of your mum's favorites." The vibrant blues and greens shimmered in the sun. "They're a bit like the paua shell your dad's gone to get for you."

Jonty rolled his lips together and tilted his head to one side as he lifted his lashes to her. There was a spark she hadn't seen before, and her stomach lurched.

"And it looks silky. I bet it feels lovely on your skin." Her fingertips pulsed with the need to touch. But she mustn't scare him. Still holding the rope in one hand, his father at the end of it, he passed the scarf to her but didn't let go. As she touched the fabric, a powerful sense of connection flowed into her. A knot of grief unraveled, hard and brittle memories disintegrated. Through misted vision, she smiled at him. He held the other end of the scarf in a chubby grip as the yacht gently rocked them. His lips lifted, and the breeze tossed his curls about. The simplicity of the moment wrapped around her and she willed it to go on forever. His childhood innocence and trust was touching a wound she'd never thought would heal.

She paused, savoring the perfect memory. "I wonder if you'd like to go to the New Year's pageant, Jonty? Your Dad used to love being part of it. I know Louis's been in it since he was six and he loves it. Maybe we could go to one of the practices with him."

A small frown pulled on Jonty's face, so she knew he was listening.

"Hey!" Cy's voice carried clear across the water. Ellie let her end of the scarf drop as Jonty stood to look over the side of the boat.

She shielded her face against the sun's glare as she stood to join him. "Are you okay?"

Two heads bobbed close to them and Louis held something above his head. His thin voice carried high on the wind. "We've got your paua shell, Jonty. Man, it was so cool down there!"

Minutes later, the two of them were at the boat and Ellie helped Louis climb the ladder. He dripped a pool of water on the deck as he hopped from one foot to the other.

"Cy said we had to get an empty one." Louis panted as he pulled off his mask and snorkel, then turned the shell over and over in his hands. "He said we shouldn't take anything that was alive. It was unreal. Fish coming right up to you and I even saw a big old lobster, but Cy said we couldn't take him!" He finished with an exaggerated roll of his eyes.

He handed the shell to Jonty. It was a chalky gray on one side and, on the other, iridescent blue and green. Jonty turned it over and over as Louis chatted about all the things he'd seen and that Cy would polish the inside so it sparkled.

Ellie dried Louis's hair with a towel and marveled at his easygoing nature. It didn't seem to bother him at all that the conversation was one-sided.

"Can we have some of those cookies you brought, Aunt Ellie? I'm starving."

She laughed. "Sure, but get changed while you're there so you don't get too cold." The younger boy followed Louis below deck while keeping hold of the precious shell.

Ellie turned to see Cy's smiling face at the top of the ladder, and her pulse quickened. Water dripped from his hair and his skin glowed.

"God, that was good," he said. He hauled himself over the side. "How's J?" He peeled the wetsuit top from his muscular torso and stood, half-naked, in front of her, water trailing down the dark hair below his belly button.

"Good. Fine," she said, her voice breathy. Her eyes wouldn't obey her mind and remained on his body as he bent to take the flippers off. His biceps jumped as he strained, and Ellie took an extra breath as her blood ran hot.

An image of the last time she was on this boat hit like an express train. The way her heart had nearly exploded when she'd reached across and kissed him, the way it had swooped when he'd kissed her back, the way her skin had sizzled as his fingers explored her body…

God, she wanted him. Wanted his arms wrapped around her body, his lips against her neck. A depth charge of need powered through her and air seized her lungs.

"It was beautiful down there."

She took a step back and held onto the railing. Did he remember? Did the memory still do to his body what it did to hers? Did he want her as much as she wanted him now?

"Are you okay?" Concern clouded his features.

"Yes." Cool steel against her palm. "Just a bit seasick while we're anchored. Are we still going to the island?"

He grinned. "Sure. Give me a minute to get dried." He went to the back of the boat, behind an inconveniently placed sail, and stripped off his wetsuit.

"Aunt Ellie?" Louis came up from below with a cookie in his mouth, Jonty following. His voice was uncharacteristically low. "Can Jonty be in the New Year's pageant with me?"

Ellie looked toward Cy, but he hadn't heard.

"I don't know, honey. I'm not sure Jonty would like that. Maybe he'd rather just watch, but we can ask his dad."

"He *wants* to be in it, don't you, Jonty? Like your dad used to be." The other boy's large, endless eyes looked up at her and he nodded. How on earth Louis had worked all that out from Jonty, she didn't know.

"Okay, we'll check with Cy." Ellie took a step on the deck before Jonty laid his arm on hers and solemnly shook his head.

"What is it, love? You don't want your dad to know?"

"It's gonna be a surprise," Louis said in a forced whisper. He put another cookie in his mouth and chewed. "Mum's gonna take me to pageant practice today, so Jonty can watch and see if he likes it, and if he does, he can be in it. Mrs. Rehua says we need some more people for the Fie Nally bit."

Ellie's heart warmed at Louis's positivity and innocence. Jonty might've responded to her today, but she couldn't see him wanting to be involved in the pageant with singing and dancing and a lot of noisy children. Cy's warning about him being pushed too much was still fresh in her mind. "If Jonty wants to go today, then that sounds like a great idea, but his dad might want to go with him."

Jonty placed a hand on the cotton of Ellie's blouse, his palm warm against her skin. She looked down into his pleading face and without hesitation answered the question she saw there. "Okay. I'll do my best to convince him."

Fifteen minutes later, Ellie and Cy sat on the pepper-and-salt sand of the tiny island and watched Jonty and Louis fly their kites in the distance. Cy's hair had dried from the slick mass of minutes ago to curls, which danced in the wind. He'd raced up and down the beach until both boys had their kites in the air and now he was breathing heavily. His glasses covered his eyes and a small crust of salt tipped the stubble on his cheeks. She tried not to look at his washboard abs narrowing to his bright blue swim shorts.

She pushed her legs out in front of her and wiggled her toes in the beautifully hot sand. "I'd say that was a pretty successful morning all round."

Cy lay flat on his back, then turned his face to hers and his mouth kicked up in a grin. "Can you believe how well Jonty and Louis are getting on?"

She smiled softly. "I know, and have you listened to the way Louis speaks to J? He never asks him a question, never expects a response. I wonder if he's comfortable with Jonty's silence because he's an only child. Growing up, he only had Fleur and our family, not a sibling or even a cousin to talk or listen to."

"He's a great kid." He shifted his body until he supported himself on an arm. "You were always a good listener. When Mum and Dad got into one of their fights, you'd always listen."

She smiled, touched by his memory, despite the fact that wasn't what happened at all. "Cy, you never used to tell me stuff about your parents. You'd come racing up to our house and say 'Wanna go and surf off the point?' I could see what had happened, but you'd never talk about it. After a whole day of silence and surfing, you'd come back to our place for dinner and mum was always worried that your parents didn't know where you were."

He shrugged. "That's what happened? I could've sworn I told you everything." His tone softened, and he twisted toward her more. "What you said back on the boat about not wanting to have children. Does that have something to do with William?"

She shielded her eyes and watched the boys, Jonty running with the string and Louis racing after him with a kite. The way small people could get beyond barriers, treat each other like friends right from the outset, was an inspiration. "Maybe."

"You think you don't *deserve* children?"

The hairs on the back of her neck stood up. "What do you mean?"

"Because you still hold yourself responsible for what happened to William, do you feel as though you don't have the right to want them?"

She scooped up a handful of sand and let the hot grains sift through her fingers, the truth in his words searing her ears. She swallowed past the lump in her throat, but she couldn't reply.

As if he sensed the raw nerve he'd touched, his voice softened. "I don't think you should be so hard on yourself, Ellie. You're great with kids, and the more time you spend with Jonty, I'm sure you'll see that."

"I guess work's become my baby," she said, shrugging. "Helping people hold on to their history. There's nothing I'd rather be doing."

"But a family. Yours was such a great one. Wouldn't you want that for yourself as well? Your own special history."

He didn't understand. She'd made a deal with herself that she'd honor William's life by giving up her own to help people hold on to their memories. He was right, she didn't deserve a child of her own, but she'd never say that out loud.

Silence stretched between them until he finally spoke again. "Kinda doesn't make sense really, you with your great family and not wanting to have kids, and me with my messed-up one and wanting to scrape a new one together. I only hope I don't screw it up."

She turned to him. "You're not screwing it up. Jonty adores you."

He scrubbed a hand through his hair. "I don't know. Sometimes I'm not sure how hard to push him. Whether he's behaving like a regular six-year-old, or if it's because of what he's been through."

"He looks like a pretty regular six-year-old right now," she said, grinning. Both boys were looking at a kite on the sand and playing with the tail.

Cy turned to her and smiled. "Shall we go see what they're doing?"

She nodded and stood, and they walked side by side across the sand.

"We can't get it up, Cy," Louis said as he held up the bright yellow kite. "I think its tail's gone wrong."

"Let me look." Cy took the kite from Louis and she watched as he untangled the tail. He pushed his sunglasses onto his head to inspect it and she couldn't pull her gaze from the rugged set of his jaw and the dimple that dug into his cheek as he talked to the boys.

"J's a good runner, but we can't launch it properly," Louis said when Cy had handed the kite back.

Cy nodded, then turned to Ellie and threw her a wink that flew straight into her heart. "Why don't we let Jonty and Ellie hold the kite up and then you and I can do the pulling? If we turn around this way so we have the wind ready to help us lift it, we might get it to work."

"Yeah, cool."

Jonty took the kite from Louis and handed it to Ellie. His cheeks were pink from running and the scarf lay loose around his neck like a fighter pilot's.

Cy took the reel, and together, he and Louis walked away until there was a long stretch of string between them.

"Do you want me to hold the kite?" Ellie said.

Jonty nodded.

"Okay, we're ready," she called on the wind. "On three we'll run. One, two, *three!*"

They jogged along the sand, Ellie with the kite held high, Jonty beside her, his arms pumping as he tried to keep up. Ahead of them, Cy and Louis had their backs turned, their hair whipping in the wind.

"Nearly ready," Ellie called to Jonty as she felt the wind beneath the kite's light material. "Ready, set, go!" And as she slowed her steps and Jonty drew up beside her, they tipped their faces skyward and watched the bright yellow smudge dancing against brilliant blue.

"What do you think, Jonty?" Cy knelt in front of his son later that afternoon. Louis jumped up and down as if he was about to burst and Jonty looked from Ellie to Louis and back again, his face shining. Fleur waited to take the boys to pageant practice. If he agreed. The connection with Ellie had been so strong today, and the prospect of being alone with her for an hour or two sent an unbidden thrill through him.

He brushed sand from the front of his little boy's T-shirt, perplexed at how this plan had come about. When they'd been heading home on the yacht, Louis had asked if Jonty could go to the practice and, to his amazement, Jonty had nodded furiously in agreement. He cleared his throat and looked into his son's expectant face. "Are you sure you want to go with Fleur and Louis? I could come too so we can see what it's like together if you like."

Jonty shook his head. Contradiction warred within Cy, wanting to keep his little boy safe and wanting to be alone with Ellie. It was one thing Jonty having new experiences, but was he ready to let his son go off with other people who might not recognize the signs of a panic attack was another.

"Hang on a minute." He indicated to Ellie and Fleur that he needed to speak to them, and they walked out of the boys' earshot. Jonty was pointing out paua shells in the steps to Louis.

Cy rubbed his hand across his chin and turned to Fleur. "Are you sure you're okay to take him? You'd need to look for any signs that he's stressed, keep him with you at all times, and send someone to get me if anything goes wrong. He hasn't been around lots of kids in a long time."

Fleur nodded. "He seems good when he's with Louis, but come if you want to."

"They'll be fine, Cy." Ellie laid a hand on his arm. "It's only down the beach and you saw how excited both boys were when Louis asked about it. Maybe a little independence will be good for J. Look how well he did when he was alone on the boat with me. Good things are happening for him."

He looked at Ellie, and she squeezed his arm as he looked into her smiling eyes. "Katie Newport will be there," she said. "Fleur can send her straight down here if something goes wrong."

"Okay." He pushed away the memory of Jonty's reaction at the glow-worms, and the guilt that he was putting his needs before his son's. "Thanks for doing this, Fleur.

When he'd waved his son goodbye, Cy watched him follow Louis like a little shadow down the beach, ducking in and out of driftwood piles. When Cy looked at Ellie, a smile touched her face, and he knew that wanting to be alone with her wasn't wrong.

"I understand that's a big step, letting him go like that." Her voice was soft, and she held his gaze seconds longer before turning back to the house.

He climbed the stairs after her and shrugged his worry

away. "I know he'll be fine with Fleur, but I don't understand why he didn't want me there."

She looked at him over her shoulder, an impish grin sparking her features. It looked perfect on her.

"I'll have to tell him about the wedding sometime soon. He'll need to be with us at the registry office, of course. I was thinking since he's starting to be more relaxed that I might tell him after Christmas. What do you think?"

"Whatever you think's best. How much will you tell him?"

He took off his denim jacket and threw it on the couch. "I'm not sure yet. I don't want to lie, but I also don't want him to think we're going to be together forever. I'll have to think about it. Hey, I've got a couple bottles of bubbles on ice for Christmas Day. What say we open one now? To celebrate all the new beginnings we have to look forward to. I can go get another one from Tom tomorrow."

She grinned as her eyes sparkled. "Go on then. There's so much to do before tomorrow, I'll need to stay up all night, anyway."

After he'd retrieved the wine from the fridge, Cy popped the cork and poured the fizzing liquid into two glasses. Ellie still sat at the table, but now her bare feet were propped on a chair opposite, her slim ankles crossed. He handed her a glass, and she grinned. "Here's to Jonty and you and to another fifty years of Rata Cove."

He touched her glass with his. "And to the woman who's guaranteed a perfect future for all three."

A smile bracketed her mouth. "And old times." She put the glass to her lips and drank.

He swallowed a mouthful of champagne, and as rivers of warmth flowed with it through his body, the tension of letting his son go to the practice lifted from his shoulders.

He nodded and placed his glass on the table. "Tell me. How was Jonty while I was snorkeling?" He topped up her glass and waited for the corners of her mouth to drop and the lines on her face to draw deeper. But neither happened. Instead, the smile touching her face grew wider as she cradled the glass in her hands.

"It was amazing."

He straightened in his chair. "Amazing?" Sudden excitement burned. He'd presumed they'd have sat looking at each other. "Did he—" Cy shook his head. No, he couldn't let himself hope it. "Did he...say something?"

"No, he didn't speak, but somehow we had a conversation. About his mum's scarf and what her favorite colors might've been."

He couldn't stop watching the light dancing on her face and the sweet lift of her lips.

"About what's scary when you're six years old and the things we've both done to make ourselves feel better."

"Really? You talked about all that with him?" His heart beat higher in his body, and bright rays of hope surged beneath his skin. He wanted to grab her hand, lace his fingers through hers, and share this experience, share the connection she'd made with his son.

"And more." Her tone was impish. "But I can't tell you what they were. A girl has to keep a secret if she's asked to. It's important to do the right thing."

"Perhaps I should do the right thing and reply to your toast." He held up the glass and waited for her to bring her hand closer. "To us, and how little we've changed."

"To us?" Her chin lifted and her lips parted. She shook her head slightly. "You really don't think we've changed?" Her voice was low.

He watched her mouth, champagne-moist, and took a

swig of his own, the cool, fizzing liquid stinging his throat as he swallowed. "You haven't changed at all."

She put her mouth to the glass but kept her eyes on his and something punched him way down deep.

It was a lie, and she knew it.

Instead of the young and vulnerable girl he used to know, now a strong and independent—sexy—woman sat before him. She swallowed her mouthful and the smooth movement of liquid sliding down her throat drew his stare to her slender neck and the vanilla skin shimmering there. He'd kissed that skin once and could remember the sweet taste of it. But what would it taste like now? Now that she was a woman who'd no doubt had a number of lovers, a woman who'd know what she wanted.

Back then, she'd been comfortable, safe. She'd changed all right, more than he'd thought possible, and it was playing hell with his focus.

"I'd like to have changed," she said softly, snapping him out of his thoughts.

"Why?"

She took another mouthful of the wine and slowly swirled it around her mouth, the sultry movement of her lips mesmerizing him.

Hot need beat down low and he crunched his stomach muscles tight. No. He couldn't. Wouldn't. If he got too close to Ellie right now, he'd end up hurting her and screwing with Jonty's life. He wouldn't let either of those things happen. When the custody was assured, it would be a different story. Then he could put his energies into winning her back for real.

"If I'd changed, I wouldn't be scared anymore."

He tried, but he couldn't make himself look past her. He

set his glass on the polished tabletop and thought he heard her take a deeper breath.

Moving to get up, she knocked her glass from the table with her elbow. It smashed into a thousand pieces on the floor; the tinkle echoing around the room like a choir. Startled, she stood and took a step toward him and, unthinkingly, he reached for her.

"I'm sorry."

"It's okay."

Her eyes were wide and infinite. Only inches away.

"What wouldn't you be scared of if...you'd changed?" he whispered, his mind spinning.

Her tongue ran across her bottom lip, and then she drew it between her teeth before releasing it. "Not scared of failing people. Not scared that if I didn't do the right thing, somebody would take the things I love away." She looked away from him. The meaning beneath her words scrambled in his ears. Did she still love him? God, his brain was so heated he wasn't sure. Hadn't she only agreed to marry him to pay him back for the secret he'd kept for her? Leaning closer, his throat closed, but his senses stood to attention and he smothered the warning in his head.

"Would you be scared of what would happen if I kissed you now?" He rasped the words out but instead of leaning into him, she stayed there, inches away, looking directly into his face and sending fingers of heat through him.

He stayed rigid, knowing this shouldn't happen, that he'd been tempted once before by her and didn't follow through. One kiss wouldn't be enough... Looking down at her glossy hair, her perfect nose, and the pout of her lips, every cell in his body ached to be nearer. Her amber eyes sparked as he reached out and traced the soft skin of her cheek.

His head told him to stay where he was, not to bend and remove the inch it would take for his lips to touch hers. That this was madness.

His body had other ideas.

An explosion of need ripped through him and he claimed her mouth with his own. The pressure of her lips against his was sweetly firm. Her breath whispered softly across his face, her palms pressed against his chest before she pulled back, leaving them both gasping.

There was nothing comfortable or safe about Ellie Jacobs anymore, and it scared the living daylights out of him.

8

---

*E*llie stepped back and shook her head. "No, Cy."

His chest constricted and instinctively he stepped closer as confusion painted her face.

"This wasn't...I'm not..." Her words wobbled as she touched her hands to her face. "I said I'd marry you, but this wasn't part of the deal."

His throat was so dry. He had to swallow before he could get it to work. "What if we changed the deal?"

"It's what we agreed, Cy," she said, but a flush bloomed from her neck up to her cheeks.

His fingertips tingled with the need to touch her, to feel her skin. "Maybe I want more."

His breath caught at the beauty of the idea. Why *shouldn't* they have more? They were adults, with their eyes open. He knew she still wanted him, had caught her looking at him. More could be better. Could take their arrangement to another level.

"More?" she said faintly.

He stepped closer, till he could feel her body heat. "Tell me you don't want more, Ellie."

Her voice wavered. "A summer fling, a bit of kissing practice so people will believe we have a genuine relationship like we had on the beach today?" She shook her head. "You haven't thought this through."

Thinking? If he were in control of his mind and body when he was around her, this wouldn't be happening. "Ellie, it's not about anything other than me wanting to kiss you."

She shifted as if to leave, then looked directly in his face. "For the here and now? For the next two weeks? Trying to get closer to me so our relationship will seem more authentic and you can be more sure of getting what you want isn't what I signed up for." Her words were rapid fire. "I've lied as much as I'm going to in my life. I'm not going to pretend we can have a real relationship when I know we can't."

"Ellie, that's *not* what's happening here. I'd never try to seduce you to get something I wanted. I'd never hurt you."

Her wild honey eyes flashed as the bald truth hit him. Of *course* he had the power to hurt her. He'd done it before. Once. And even though he'd left to spare her the weight of him wanting to tell, and she wanting to keep their secret, he'd never forgotten the pain on her face or the tears on her cheeks.

She said nothing for a moment, then moved to the fireplace and picked up the dustpan and brush. "You're just getting carried away in the moment."

"Ellie..."

She began vigorously sweeping the pieces of glass into the dustpan, a loose ringlet falling across her face. "There's too much history between us, Cy, too much hurt for us to get over. If that kiss is some sort of apology—"

"Trying to fix what happened in the past is not why I kissed you now."

She shook her downcast head. "You're under a lot of stress. You kissed me because we have unfinished business. Things didn't end the way they should have between us, but now we owe it to ourselves and Jonty to start fresh."

"You mean you don't feel the same connection I feel to you? I can't believe that."

"I don't believe you really feel a connection," she said, her tone softening. "You want the situation with Jonty to work out so badly that you'll do whatever it takes, but this isn't a game. I haven't offered you my body or my heart."

Tiny furrows scarred her brow and his gut hollowed out. He reached for the dustpan. "I'll take that." She looked away as he took the broken glass from her and emptied it in the kitchen. He steeled himself as he came into the living room. She was right; he could screw everything up if he wanted something and she didn't. Imagine if this spooked her into withdrawing her agreement to marry him.

"I'm sorry, Ellie, but I can't help how I feel, and I'm pretty damn sure you feel it too."

Her shoulders slumped.

He pushed out a sharp breath as he steadied himself against the lintel. She still had to know there was no hidden agenda. "I kissed you now because it felt right." He took a step forward as a rush of awareness trapped him. "I kissed you because I was sick of imagining it every time I'm with you."

"You're hurting, Cy." She leaned on an old bookshelf, her face soft but resigned. "You've come back here to find reassurance that some parts of your life are the same as they always were." The caring in her tone unraveled him. "But they're not. I'm not. Long term, I don't want to be a wife and mother. I've built a life for myself, something I'm not going to abandon for a flimsy relationship founded on deception and disappointments. I've agreed to marry you and live with you for one year and that's all. That's all I have to give."

A sharp pain dug into his chest and he pressed the wood of the doorway beneath his fingertips. "I know you're not the same."

"We've both moved on to incredibly different places in our lives. We're just going to end up hurting each other, and more importantly Jonty, if we pretend otherwise." She waved her hand across her lips as if dismissing the tingle still radiating in his. "You're trying to make something out of a relationship that can never be."

The words slapped him, and he shook his head. She thought he was manipulating her. It was sketched in the lines by her mouth and the shadows on her face. He wasn't wrong. He was certain she still felt something for him. But having Ellie to help fight for his son was way more important than having her in his arms. He had to remember that or everything could fall apart.

"Okay," he said. "If you're not ready to acknowledge what's happening between us, I'll respect that, but I can't ignore the way I feel."

Ellie sank down onto the sofa and dropped her head into her hands. She'd only been back from Cy's for half an hour and her legs were still jelly, her skin still hummed. For so long she'd imagined being that close to him again, savoring the feel of his lips on hers, sinking into his strong arms, but she'd been surprised by the intensity of her reaction.

He was desperate. She got that, but he needed to know she'd worked too hard on her happiness in the last few years to throw it all away on a quick fling. Whether he'd kissed her because he hadn't thought through what it might mean for her, or because some real reaction from her might help when he was faking the kiss in public, she wasn't sure.

Whatever the reason, deep down she knew that part of him hadn't changed. She still sensed something coiled inside Cy, like he was ready to bolt at any minute. The way he'd reacted at the glow-worms was a prime example of how he pushed others away when things got difficult.

"Ellie! Ellie! Where are you?" Fleur's voice flew across the garden from the gate.

Jonty. Ellie rushed onto the deck to meet her, heart pounding. "What's wrong?"

"Oh. My. God." Fleur panted, red-faced as she ran onto the deck, her flip-flops in her hand. Louis, as usual, swaggered behind. "You won't believe it, Ell." She put a palm flat on her chest as if to slow her heart. "He talked." Her eyes shone as they widened.

"Really? That's incredible!"

She collapsed into a chair, breathing heavily, and Ellie sat down next to her, heart still racing. *The miracle Cy's been waiting for.*

"Well, he didn't actually talk, but he *sang*. He sang with all the kids when they were onstage doing, *A Pukeko in a Ponga Tree*." Her words ran into each other as she rushed on.

"Cyndi Rehua was teaching everyone the words to the final song and when she told them about the last line, 'A Pukeko in a Ponga Tree,' he got all excited and started squirming in his chair. Louis told Cyndi about Jonty's little pukeko chick, so Cyndi said if we could find a toy pukeko, he could hold it and be the *ponga* tree in the pageant. He went up onstage with Louis, and then he started singing with the other kids!"

Fleur paused and chewed her lip. "Well, I don't actually

know if he made any *noise*, but he definitely mouthed all the words and did all the actions."

Ellie leaned forward as Louis ambled past them into the house. She was desperate for every last detail. "What did Cy say when you dropped Jonty off? He'd have been over the moon." If only she could've seen his face. If she hadn't left so quickly, she could've seen his joy.

Fleur hesitated. "I didn't tell him."

"You what? How could you not tell him something so huge?"

Fleur tucked her legs under her. "I said to Jonty on the way out, 'Wait till we tell your dad,' and he and Louis started jumping up and down." She shrugged. "God knows how Louis understands, it's like they've got a secret language, but he said that Jonty wants it to be a surprise for his dad. He doesn't want Cy to know about the performance until New Year's Eve."

Ellie leaned back and nodded. "I told Jonty about the pageant, how his dad had loved being in it and it seemed to touch something in him." She remembered his shining face and blossoming smile. "How can we keep it a secret from Cy, though? Jonty will have to go to practice every day for a week."

Fleur grinned. "I thought about that. We can take the boys to practice. Make some excuse about Cy not needing to come. He'll think it's some sort of hero worship Jonty's got for Louis anyway, so we can pretend that's what's happening."

Ellie blew out a breath. "It will be an amazing surprise."

"He'll be fine," her sister said. "Honestly, I think part of that little guy's problem is that he can sense Cy's fear. A few interactions with other people away from his dad might be what he needs."

Jonty deserved fun and happiness, and it was lovely he'd found some in Rata Cove. A spark raced through her and she couldn't help but smile. She could only imagine the shock on Cy's face when he saw Jonty up onstage on New Year's Eve.

Fleur tilted her head to one side and shot her sister a look from under her lashes. "Speaking of surprises, there was an empty champagne flute on the table at Cy's place and he told me to be careful where I walked because another got smashed." Her eyes narrowed. "Funny, don't you think?"

Crawling heat spread across Ellie's face. Ignoring Fleur's penetrating stare, Ellie smiled and looked away.

"You still look good together, Ellie, and it's nice that you've rekindled your friendship. People won't have such a hard time believing you're in love."

Ellie: *So, I just wanted you both to know that I said yes to Cy's proposal...*

Kirin: *Holy crap, I did NOT see that coming.*

Gwin: *Oh, wow. Sending you enormous hugs from Brentwood Bay. I know how massive that decision must have been for you.*

Ellie: *Thanks, knowing I've got you guys to talk to makes everything easier.*

Kirin: *Are you feeling good now that you've decided?*

Ellie: *Well, I was until Cy tried to kiss me.*

She added a row of worried face emojis.

Gwin: *And how did that turn out?*

Ellie: *Even though I could have gone on kissing him all afternoon, I stopped it. I told him that making a move on me wasn't* *part of the agreement and that he was only doing it out of a sense of gratitude.*

Kirin: *So you were tempted to take it further?*

Ellie: *Absolutely I was tempted. Cy is gorgeous and kind, and he makes my heart do a backwards somersault. He knows the deepest parts of me. . .But things are complicated enough.*

Gwin: *It's kinda understandable that it happened, I guess. He must be so relieved you've agreed to the proposal. And it's Christmas. Everything seems a bit surreal at Christmas.*

Kirin: *Everyone goes **nuts** at Christmas.*

Ellie: *And there was a glass or two of champagne involved.*

Gwin: *Emotions and bubbly wine? Lethal combination.*

Kirin: *And you know, maybe the kiss **needed** to happen. For you both to acknowledge that there's still attraction there, but now you've made it clear why pursuing that would be a bad idea.*

Ellie: *Only problem is I'm now going to spend half my time pretending that there **is** a physical connection between us—so that people really think we're together—while trying to deny it to myself when we **are** together.*

Kirin: *Well, I see it as a good thing.*

Ellie: *Really? How can it be good that the man who clearly only wants to pretend that we're together, kisses me when there's absolutely no reason to?*

Kirin: *No reason other than the fact that he's not thinking straight. I'm sure that when he realizes how stupid it was, he'll never try it again. There's just too much on the line for all of you for him to risk it again.*

Gwin: *Kirin's right. He'd be risking you backing out of the agreement and he's never going to let that happen.*

Ellie: *Oh God, this is so complicated! I took this job thinking it would be a working holiday, and it's quickly turning into something I never imagined.*

Kirin: *You've made your position really clear to Cy now.*

That you don't want anything to happen between you. I see it as a line in the sand. He's not going to cross that again.

Ellie: *Yeah, maybe you're right. Maybe having that out in the open will make things easier from now on.*

Gwin: *I think so.*

Kirin: *So what happens now?*

Ellie: *Now we get through Christmas and in the new year we get married at a registry office in Auckland. And then we leave for the States. . .*

Kirin: *And then the three of us can meet up! When everything's sorted for you, I'm going to hatch a plan for us all to get together. I want to hug you both in person for helping me so much with the inferno that was my life.*

Ellie: *That sounds amazing. I'll go wherever I need to see you beauties in person. It'll be great to have that to look forward to.*

Gwin: *Amen to that. Ellie, I know things will be fine and that you're going to make this work because you've weighed up the pros and cons, and you're just such a good person.*

They continued chatting for a while longer, Gwin and Kirin asking her what a summer Christmas was like, and then all of them making plans for how they could meet up when Ellie was back in the States.

She was feeling better now. Kirin and Gwin were right—she and Cy had acknowledged that there was still a physical connection between them—but now they understood why they couldn't act on it. At least she hoped Cy felt the same way.

Christmas Day.

The thought tumbled over and over in Ellie's head as she woke hot and sticky the next morning, a sheet wrapped around her middle. She'd been dreaming about making love to Cy in a tent in the desert. He'd been a sheik in flowing robes and somehow she'd got tangled up in them. She squeezed her eyes tight and buried her head in the pillow. That was *not* the sort of dream she should've been having after their argument last night.

The dull light indicated it was still very early, but there was a noise outside her room. Banging. *Thwump, thwump,* over and over.

She dragged her head up and listened. Yes, banging—coming from the living room. Suddenly, her door opened and Fleur's smiling face appeared. "You might want to get up. Seems Santa's been, and he brought weapons."

Ellie pulled on a bathrobe and slid her bedroom door open before she'd had time to wake properly. "What time is it?" she managed through a dry mouth. "Is the sun up? I thought a couple of possums—"

"Merry Christmas!"

Her stomach pitched. Cy, Jonty, and Louis sat on the floor with wrapping paper scattered around them. She pulled a hand through her hair and her fingers snagged in the unruly mess. What was Cy doing here? On Christmas morning? In her living room?

She hadn't seen him yesterday, but the brand on her lips from where he'd kissed her the day before flamed and her knees went weak. The thin cotton of her nightgown seemed too little protection as her body hummed with the memory. If she looked into his eyes, she might burst into flames.

"Look what Santa brought, Aunt Ellie!" Louis spoke, rapid-fire. "He must've found out I'm friends with J now 'cause he brought us both terror swords!"

"Terror what?"

"A terror sword. Look!" He waved around an enormous gray sword with flashing lights. "This is the other half of Jonty's one and when you use them together, they know what moves the other one's doing."

The bulging Christmas stocking at Louis's feet was barely visible under red-and-gold wrapping paper. The toys looked expensive, and there was no way Fleur could have afforded such a thing. Cy must have brought them. A curl of gratitude unwound in her chest. Cy had been unsure about Jonty's first Christmas in New Zealand, and now he'd made it extra special for both boys.

Louis jumped up in his racing car pajamas. "Come on, J. Let's show Ellie."

Jonty hopped up, too, and like a couple of samurai warriors, the boys thumped the swords against each other and recorded sounds of metal clashing, fighter jets screaming, and cows mooing filled the room.

"Wow!" Ellie laughed. "I've never seen such fabulous swords, have you, Cy?"

She turned toward him and when he looked across at her he grinned, his eyes sparking bright with the same desire she'd seen there two days ago.

"We thought Santa was pretty sharp finding out that these two are friends," he said.

"I had heard that Santa's pretty smart." A smile tugged her mouth.

Fleur came in with coffees. "I'm going into the bush out back to cut some *pohutukawa* blossoms for the table decoration. I'll take the boys with me so the neighbors don't think someone's being drawn and quartered. Is that okay, Cy?"

A shadow passed across his face and he hesitated before

saying, "Sure. We'll come out when we've finished the coffee."

"Sorry you missed the opening of the stockings," he said when Fleur had gone outside. "As soon as Jonty opened his presents at home, he got dressed and headed out the door, wanting to see what Louis got. I don't know if you noticed, but this is the first time since he's been here that he hasn't worn his scarf."

"Oh, Cy that's fantastic!"

"It's still in his back pocket, but I think there's so much going on here that he's happy to focus on other things. I was about to knock on your door when we arrived, but the boys were too quick. I told them we had to wait until dinner for the rest of the presents." He threw her a lopsided grin that alighted on her skin. The thumping of the swords faded into the distance as the boys moved off the deck.

"Thanks for doing that for Louis." Ellie busied herself tidying wrapping paper so she didn't have to look at him, but her heart softened at his thoughtfulness. "Money's pretty tight for Fleur."

Cy swiped the air. "It's nothing. He's a great kid, and he's been great for Jonty. Katie went into Papaatawhai for me and got everything yesterday."

She reached for the coffee. "Want one?"

"Sure," he said, and she passed him the steaming cup.

"I want to apologize for the other day."

"We need sugar." She swiveled abruptly and walked into the kitchen in search of the sugar, heat flooding her cheeks. God, why was she reacting like this?

"Ellie?"

She stilled, trying to reconcile her reaction to him. Straightening her spine, she found a neutral expression and turned.

He stood in the middle of the tiny living room, one hand slung in his shorts pocket, the other dragging across his chin. "Thursday..." He cleared his throat. "It was a perfect day. A perfect day that I should've put an end to about half an hour earlier."

"So why didn't you?" She stood frozen to the spot and realized she was holding her breath.

He lifted a shoulder and let it fall. "I'm not sure, really. Maybe relief that things were panning out so well. Maybe nostalgia and the fact that I still feel close to you. But those two things are all about me. I wasn't thinking enough about you."

She blinked and moistened her lips. "As I said, it's an emotional time, but it's other people we need to pretend for, not each other." She tried to make her voice sound light. "The only future you and I have is the next year, and our focus has to be Jonty. After that, I'm going to get on with what I was doing before you came back here, trying to build my business so I can stay in New Zealand. I know you've explained why you had to leave back then, but it doesn't undo the fact you hurt me and I won't let that happen again."

He held her gaze for a long moment and then nodded. "I hope we can put it behind us and get on with enjoying Christmas then."

Put it behind them. It was exactly what they needed to do. What she had to do. So why was her chest so tight that she could barely draw breath?

"There's not going to be a Christmas if I don't get dressed. There's the turkey to put on, the peas to shell. And I have a whole lot of potatoes that need to be scrubbed if you're up for it."

He pulled her close and hugged her. "Sounds perfect."

"Whew, I'm stuffed!" Louis pushed his empty dessert plate away and slumped against the back of his chair. The sparkly wrap and dubious innards from Christmas crackers lay strewn across the table and the white cloth was stained with red wine and grape juice. A heat haze of roast dinner and burning sun hovered in the air.

Cy stood and slapped a fist on his chest. "Time to do the rest of these dishes, men. Looks like these ladies could do with a snooze."

Louis turned a stricken face to his mother. "Can Jonty and I go test our new skimboards, Mum? We need to do it before everyone goes down for the cricket. Promise we'll help clean up later."

"Maybe Ellie and Cy will go watch you while I finish up these plates."

Ellie looked out across the deck to where the distant ocean had left shallow pools across the sand. "Are you sure? I'm happy to stay and do dishes."

"I want to start my new book, so some peace and quiet would be nice. You guys go." Fleur stood and began taking dishes into the kitchen.

Ellie turned to Cy. "I'll go if you want to have a snooze. Three helpings of pavlova might stop you moving for a little while."

Cy laughed and his eyes shone. "I could do with a bit of a run around on the beach."

Louis rolled his eyes. "We don't need any grown ups to come down."

Picking up her glass of water, Ellie threw a look at Cy before smiling at Louis and Jonty. "I want to have a go on one of those skim boards, too. Go and get your sunscreen on, and some hats."

Louis and Jonty rushed about getting things together and a few minutes later, the four of them were walking across the sand to the shallow pools of water in the distance, the boys in front with skim boards tucked under their arms.

Cy turned to her. "I know you said all that stuff on the boat and the island about not wanting to have your own kids, but you really are great with them."

Goose bumps flitted across her skin at the softness of his tone and Ellie grinned. "When I decided not to have my own kids, I made a pact with myself to be the best aunt I possibly could."

He shook his head, but his focus was still on the boys ahead.

"The best part is, I can remind Louis about all the things his mum wants done, but I can spoil him rotten as well."

Cy stopped walking and put a hand in his pocket. "He loves that watch you gave him."

Ellie stopped too and raised her hand to shield the sun from her eyes as she watched the boys. "He spotted it in a jeweler's store window when he stayed with me once. I offered to clean the glass because he'd pressed his nose up against it so long."

Cy was holding out a small package in the palm of his hand. A bright pink ribbon trailed over purple paper.

"What's this?"

His mouth lifted in a soft smile. "I should've put it under the tree, but it might've been crushed in the boy stampede."

Her face heated as she touched her fingers against her lips. "Oh, Cy. I didn't get you anything."

"You've given me more than enough. You've guaranteed

the rest of our lives are filled with happier times. That's the only gift I wanted. Merry Christmas, Ellie."

Holding her breath, she pulled the ribbon. It gave way and the paper beneath came unstuck. Lifting out the tiny box, she pulled the lid off with trembling fingers.

Resting on a bed of crushed tissue paper was a perfect white nautilus shell. She gasped and traced the lines, its spiraled ridges rough under her fingertips. "It's beautiful," she whispered. Where did you get it?"

He leaned forward, his voice low, and pushed his sunglasses on top of his head. "I found it when I took Louis snorkeling the other day. I thought you'd like it."

The beauty, the simplicity of his gesture, sent a river of warmth through her and a pulse beat loudly in her ears. Friends gave each other gifts. He'd given her things before. So why did this one make her breath burn in her mouth and her mind spin to their kiss yesterday? Her heart beat more quickly, but she ignored it.

She placed the lid on the box. "I'll take it back to my place in Auckland," she said, tipping her face up to his. "To wait for me till I come back home next summer."

"I was thinking you could bring it to the States with you to remind you of home," he said quietly. "The more I think about what you're doing for us, the more humbled I am. What I'm asking of you is really setting back your business plans and I want you to know I'll never forget that. I know what you're giving up for us, Ellie and I'll always be in your debt."

She forced a smile. "I'm sure I won't forget everything in a year."

"I know you won't."

Without thinking, Ellie reached for his hand. "I love the shell. It's beautiful." She rose on tiptoes to place a kiss on his cheek, but something made her hesitate. His mouth was so close, so tempting. She could hear his breathing, smell the cool marine scent of him. She tilted her head and placed her lips on his.

A soft groan sounded in his throat and, on reflex, she slid her hands across his muscled shoulders, pulling him closer. Playing her tongue along his lips, she reveled in the sweetness of wine and dessert and that special taste that was all Cy. He opened his mouth to her, cupping her face in his hands.

Mindless as she kissed him deeper, sparks ignited in her blood. Cy stroked the skin of her neck and she let herself sink into the beautiful sensations rippling through her. Blood pounded in her ears, becoming louder and louder until Cy pulled suddenly away.

Jonty was standing still in front of them, his eyes wide, cheeks flushed. Cy dropped to his knees. "It's okay, bud, Ellie and I were just..."

Before he could finish, Jonty was running back up the beach, away from them. Cy stood, frozen to the spot, and then they both ran after him.

"I'll get him," Cy called as he raced ahead of Ellie.

"But I want to..."

"Just give us some time, Ellie." Strong arms pumping, his legs sprinting along the beach, he went up, over a sand dune, and disappeared.

9

—————

*L*ungs bursting, Cy slid down the sand dune until he reached waist-high sea grass at the bottom. Cutting his hands as he pushed back the long, spiky blades, he finally found his son crouched in the middle of a clearing.

God, why had he kissed Ellie? After he'd reminded himself there was too much at stake for him to act on his impulses, he'd just forgotten it all for another stolen moment with her.

Willing his blood to slow, the adrenaline to stop washing through his body, he calmed his breathing and wiped damp palms against his shorts. If he'd known where Jonty would run to, he wouldn't have followed in case it made things worse. Looking at the way his little boy was sitting frozen, staring straight ahead with the scarf back around his neck, it seemed that's exactly what had happened.

"Jonty." He moved slowly closer. "Hey, I'm sorry you were confused when you saw me kissing Ellie."

His son's large blue eyes were fixed on a bush in the distance, unblinking.

What could he say about what Ellie meant to him, what their relationship was, why he'd kissed her like that, without confusing a six-year-old further?

"I know it must seem strange, but Ellie and I have been friends for a long time. We were only a bit older than Louis is now when we first met, so we've had a lot of time to get really close."

Still, his son said nothing and Cy leaned in. Jonty's hair was mussed from all the playing with Louis today, and there was a sticky spot at the corner of his mouth where a stray piece of pavlova had landed.

"Son, there's something I need to tell you." He shuffled closer so he could sense the warmth of Jonty's body only inches away. He ached to put his arm around his boy's shoulders, but he wanted to respect the distance his son so obviously needed and jammed his hands between his own knees. "You already know Ellie's coming back home with us, right? But I also want to tell you that in a few days' time Ellie, you, and I are going to drive to the city and Ellie and I are going to get married."

He thought he felt his son stiffen, but the little boy stayed frozen to the spot.

Cy swallowed, unsure of how much to tell him, how to describe what his relationship with Ellie was. He took a deep breath of salty sea air. Man, he didn't know what his relationship with Ellie was himself, or how he'd prepare for the time she'd be leaving both of them.

"Having Ellie with us won't change the way you and I do things together, bud. We'll still have fun and do our boy things and when we get back to Colorado..."

Jonty lay on the sand, pulled his knees into his chest, and put the scarf over his mouth. Cy thought his heart would shatter. Instinctively, he reached a hand out, touched his little boy's back, and rubbed.

Had coming back to New Zealand been a monumental mistake? Thinking back to the way Jonty had come alive since they'd got here, how he'd turned from a frightened little boy to one who'd fly kites and try new things made him sure that it wasn't Rata Cove that was the problem. In fact, this place was the catalyst for his change.

And it wasn't Ellie. She'd told him how she and Jonty had connected on the boat and he'd watched them becoming closer every day.

A lead weight formed in his gut. No, it was the fact that Cy's attention was drawn away from his son. At the most pivotal time in both their lives, he was letting his physical need for Ellie take over. And her desire for him was growing, too; he could feel it. But she was already giving up so much. Her business would suffer significantly being away for a year, and if they started a relationship that fell apart later. . ?

He'd hurt her once before and he wouldn't let that happen again. No matter how much he wanted to get closer to Ellie, for her sake and for his son, he couldn't. Knowing that cut more deeply than he'd ever thought possible.

So much for second chances.

Cy was fixing the old grinder in the lean-to later that evening. He'd pulled it from the garden shed preparing to polish the paua shell he'd got for Jonty.

Rain thundered on the roof and the waves on the beach were heavier. It hadn't taken long for his son to fall asleep after they'd got home from the beach. When he'd finally felt that Jonty was ready to leave the sand dune, he'd picked him up and carried him home. They'd seen Ellie in the distance, and he'd waved to let her know everything was okay. But it wasn't. He felt an overpowering need to protect his son from anything else that was too confronting and he dreaded the trip to Auckland in two days' time when they'd organize the wedding.

A noise behind him made him swing around.

Ellie stood framed in the doorway, her hair stuck to her head, hand on her chest as she sucked in a breath. "Hi," she said as water dripped from her hair. "I got caught in the rain." She flicked water from her hands, her clothes clinging to her, accentuating every perfect curve.

"It was so hot and sticky when I set out that I didn't imagine it'd rain. Then the most enormous drops came splashing down. I'm soaked."

He picked up the towel Jonty had used earlier in the day and motioned toward her. "Come here." Her face glowed pink and tiny droplets of water sparkled on the tips of her lashes. She was breathtakingly beautiful, even with mascara smudged down her cheeks.

"Is it okay that I'm here?" she whispered. "I wanted to make sure Jonty was okay. And you. I won't stay long."

She tipped her head forward, and he captured her hair in the towel and rubbed.

"Of course it's okay. I should have texted to tell you he's settled and asleep." He finished drying her hair and eased her head back up. Her eyes were filled with concern, and he couldn't help focusing on the lips she'd pressed to his this afternoon.

She shivered.

"Come inside and warm up, and then I'll get Jonty." He

touched her shoulder. "I'll run you back to Starfish in the car."

"No, don't wake him. I'll be fine."

He shoved a hand in his pocket. "There's an old raincoat hanging by the front door. You could wear that back."

She nodded and then followed him up the steps.

When they were inside, Ellie went straight to the old fireplace, her arms crossed. "Cy, I'm so sorry Jonty saw us kissing. In fact, I'm sorry I kissed you. It made no sense after what I said to you the other day, what we agreed to this morning. I got carried away in the moment."

Cy shoved hands in the pockets of his shorts. "It's not your fault, Ellie. It's mine. I've let myself get distracted since I've been here, and it's caused me to take my eyes off Jonty. I won't let that happen again. Jonty will be fine."

She blinked and a raindrop he must have missed splashed onto her cheek like a wayward crystal. "*Will* you?"

His throat dried as he leaned against the wall. "I don't care about me. I know I have the capacity to be selfish, to focus on the things that I want, but this one time in my life I'm determined to put that aside for the good of my son."

The air hummed between them. Standing there with her damp hair and her fresh face, she could've been the eighteen-year-old he'd known in another lifetime. But now she was a woman who knew herself so well that she'd change her well-planned life to help a friend. A woman who, despite feeling uneasy around children, had worked hard to get to know his son. And she was a woman who'd seen the pain of an old friend and was prepared to do something outrageous so he could be happy.

Her face lit as she looked up at him. "Well, *I* care about you."

"You shouldn't." It wasn't meant to sound so rough. "I

wish I had half your strength, half the guts you've shown to set your chin high and get on with things." He blinked as he paused, wanting her to understand how much he meant this. "You blow me away, Ellie. The way you can talk so openly about William, the way you've dedicated your life to the happiness of other people. When I thought about asking you to marry me, it was because I had to focus on doing whatever it took to get Jonty back in my life, and I can't believe how lucky I am that you said yes."

She took a step toward him and air seemed to be sucked out of the room. "I'm not the only one who's changed, Cy. I never would've picked you as someone who'd find himself battling for his son. After everything you went through as a kid, I half expected that you'd be the one globe-trotting and staying single, not me." She took another step and every one of his cells pulled toward her as if she possessed some magnetic power.

"I guess we've both found some meaning in our lives that we're determined to hang on to," he said when she was only a touch away.

Her fingers landed on his arm with the lightest touch. "You have to be happy too, Cy." Every square inch of his skin that she touched drank her closeness. "You deserve some happiness." He let out a private sigh as the air grew heavier around him and her touch reached all the way to his heart.

Rain drummed on the roof and he covered her hand with his. Her stare pinned him to the spot and her skin grew warm beneath his fingers. No muscle in his body would move.

The set of her face changed as she drew in a breath. The smile faded, and her gaze was edged with an emotion he hadn't seen before, a shadowed look that sent shivers racing down his spine. Her lips parted and Cy's heart thumped.

Breaking the spell, he released his hand and stood back. Need for her made him light-headed, restless. Seconds of silence multiplied. The shadows on her face deepened. He'd been here before with her, this place where his blood heated and his body fired.

Despite the fright they'd all had today, she'd come here to make sure he and his son were all right. Anyone else might have run for the hills by now, but Ellie's constancy, her strength and determination, were like a drug he couldn't get enough of. There were so many reasons he shouldn't be doing this, but his ache for her and the fire licking his body were too strong to resist.

Leaning closer, he braced himself for the knockout punch to his senses, then placed his lips on hers. Blood fizzed through his veins and she stayed perfectly still, breathing him in.

Cupping her face in his hands, he pulled her closer and drew out the kiss. When her arms encircled him, he shuddered. Maybe if they gave into each other this one time, maybe if they sated their need for each other for tonight only, it would put an end to the want that had started the moment he came back here.

"Ellie," he whispered.

He threaded a hand through her hair, then ran his tongue along her bottom lip. The taste of her, cool and sweet, seeped into his mouth. Her tongue met his as he trailed his hands down the length of her back. Slowly, so slowly, he kissed along the curve of her mouth and she moaned in response.

With both hands on her back, he pulled her closer, until they were hip to hip and the fire within him flared higher. From somewhere locked deep within, a hunger to have more of her surged. Without wanting to remember the myriad reasons this was where they should stop, Cy pulled back, took Ellie's hand, and led her to the bedroom.

Ellie squeezed his hand as she followed him to the bedroom. This was just for now, and that was all. Just for one night she wanted to enjoy Cy, the way she'd always imagined as a woman she would.

The sash windows in the small room were open, curtains puffing in as the hot, damp night air rolled in from the sea. The dying glow of a bonfire on the beach and the muted light from the living room cast flickering blue shadows across everything. Cy's face was silhouetted as she looked up into it.

His breathing, soft and full, made her own breath hitch. Her mind raced forward, to being under him, part of him, and she had to close her eyes to stop herself from moaning before he'd even touched her body.

He took her other hand in his so they were face to face and slowly he inched her back across the wooden floor to the wall, his mouth getting closer to hers with every step as he dipped his face lower. Her feet were light on the polished wooden floor, as if she were floating, weightless.

Desperate to taste him again, she arched her neck up, but he stayed tantalizingly distant, teasing. The edge of his mouth was curved in a grin.

With one last step backwards, he pressed her into the wall and she waited for his lips to claim her. Her mouth heavy with need, she swallowed in anticipation of his next move.

But his face stayed inches away and slowly he lifted both

arms above her head and pinned her, palm to palm. Bodies, cruelly distant.

This wasn't the boy she remembered with his clumsy speed and sense of excitement. Not the stolen love on a random afternoon. This was the moment with the man she'd dreamed about, strong and confident, certain of what he wanted. And it caused her limbs to weaken, her lips to open, and her breasts to ache.

He leaned in so his chest was inches from hers and her nipples peaked in readiness, the fabric of her bra straining as she took a breath.

"Kiss me," she half-begged, and he leaned in and grazed her cheek with his own as he lowered his face, the stubbled pleasure and pain shooting beats of desire across her skin.

With hands above her head, body revealed, Cy claimed her mouth, and she searched the depths of his with her tongue. The taste of him was sweet as she played her tongue across his lips.

Moaning, he moved closer and pushed his knee between her legs, opening her to him and she kissed him deeper.

Achingly vulnerable with her hands above her head, Ellie writhed to get closer, but he held her hands fast.

"Stay where you are." His voice was whisper close and the confident command sent new chills across her skin.

Doing as she was told, she held her arms high as he let go and kissed a trail down her body. First her neck where his teeth nicked her skin, then down to her blouse, where he stopped and his fingers worked the buttons.

"You're beautiful," he growled. Unexpectedly, his fingers stilled on the buttons. "You're so beautiful." And the ring of sincerity in his voice made her head swim.

Blissfully, he turned his face back and in a second, her blouse was open. He left it hanging and kissed the skin above her bra, working across in fine, feathering movements until her nipples stood to attention and right to her centre she ached for him.

Unable to keep from touching him any longer, Ellie lowered her hands and rested them in his hair, feeling his movements as he kissed her back and forth.

With heated blood, she guided his head to her breast and slowly, he lowered one cup on her bra.

Prickles of desire showered her body as he gently took her in his mouth and sucked and licked until she was ready to explode.

"Shhh," he said, and she realized she'd been moaning. She needed to be in charge of her responses and the only way to do that was to take charge of Cy.

She eased his head from her breast and pulled him up and closer until she kissed him on the mouth. Desperate, she pushed him back toward the bed, the heat from the soles of her feet making her stick to the floor.

At the bed she pushed him back, further, further, until he was sitting, then lying on the soft cotton coverlet. Her breath shallow, Ellie hiked her skirt and crawled on top of him, hands supporting her on either side of his face.

Like a triumphant predator, she knelt over him, her blouse open, skin slick with desire.

"Ellie." He whispered her name as he came up for air from their kiss and tugged off her blouse. "I want you now." He moaned and flipped her under him, so his arms were on either side of her body. It was just the right angle for her to reach her hands under his t-shirt and feel the hot, tight body beneath.

Cy moaned as she played her hand along the top of his jeans before she pulled the t-shirt up and over his head. The moonlight from the window outlined Cy's naked torso above her, and Ellie immediately wanted more.

"Take off your jeans," she said.

With one hand still by her body, he undid the jeans and flicked them to the floor.

"Now you." His voice was a low growl as she kicked off her panties as he rolled to the side and reached for something on the bedside table. When he'd sheathed himself, the only thing between them was the soft cotton of her skirt and he put his hand under it, caressing her bottom. The slick between her legs and the rigid shape of him pressing against her said it was time, and she rose and drew him into her.

Filled with him, she closed her eyes, but his voice was insistent, a low, throaty rumble. "Look at me, Ellie."

The softness in his eyes pulled at her heart before he kissed her once more. As she rocked and rocked, every sense flew higher, the touch, the taste, the smell of him. And when his moans came quicker, she held him tight as pleasure bombs pounded through her and then slowly, slowly subsided.

Cy drew in scorched air as he completed another pull-up on the branch of an old rata tree behind his house the next morning. Sun beat down on his bare skin and his muscles stung. At least it masked the mess firing through his brain.

He'd made love to Ellie. Despite all his resolutions not to shift the focus, despite her warnings she wanted nothing long term, he'd given into the pull of her and they'd made love. It had been incredible, powerful. He hadn't stopped thinking about her since they'd kissed one final time in his doorway before she'd run barefoot into the darkness. And that was the problem. Every time he'd taken his focus off Jonty, his son had taken a step backward. Had he destroyed everything?

He looked down to where Jonty sat eating a bowl of cereal on a sunny patch of grass, the *crunch, crunch* blending with the screech of cicadas in the bush. Bright crimson needles from the rata flowers surrounded him like a Persian carpet.

If his son had been confused by a kiss yesterday, what could this level of connection with Ellie do to him? It was one thing to share a kiss with her from time to time, but this meant so much more. He knew they shouldn't have given in to their desires, yet he'd missed the sweet sound of her breathing and the soft touch of her skin against his after he watched her walk out the door. Were they in so deep that they'd forgotten why they were together again?

He let himself drop to the ground and reached for the towel and water bottle at his feet. "What'll we do today then, J? Want to go out on the yacht again? We could go fishing this time. Catch something for dinner." Getting away from the bay for an afternoon might help him find a way through this.

Jonty lifted his eyes as he chewed his mouthful. His little brow crumpled as he shook his head.

"Eeling then. Down at the creek. We could go and find some eels." He took a mouthful of water.

Jonty's eyes moved back to his bowl.

"We could finish polishing up the paua shell we got snorkeling."

At the sound of the gate to the beach being unlatched, Jonty dropped his bowl and spoon, then scrambled to his feet. He rounded the corner of the house in a second, his dinosaur T-shirt flapping. It would be Louis coming to find his friend. Memories of Ellie doing the exact same thing a decade ago ate at him.

"Hey, Jonty." Ellie's sweetly singsong voice tugged at him and the sweat that had cooled on Cy's skin fired again. He stood still, listening.

"I just took a look at your little pukeko. He's doing great this morning."

"Looks like his foot's all better." It was Louis's voice. There was silence for a moment, and Cy imagined the smile on his son's little face that the bird was better.

"Are you ready to come to the hall? It's a full practice today." Her voice was softer and he could imagine her smiling. "Louis's mum will meet us down at the hall 'cause she's got a few phone calls to make. Have you got your hat? I'll look around for your dad."

"Let's get your terror sword, too, and we can show the other kids," Louis said.

Thundering feet raced through the house and Cy pulled his shoulders back as he rounded the corner.

"Morning." He was afraid of what she might see in his eyes, but without his sunglasses, he had no choice but to look directly at her and the smile he found almost unbuckled him. Perfect crescents dimpled her cheeks. Why hadn't he noticed those dimples before? His mouth dried as his eyes drifted to hers and the memory of her kissing him and holding him close sent warmth feathering through his veins.

"Hi." She rubbed the side of her neck.

He took a mouthful of water from the bottle and let the liquid cool every heated part of him. Her reaction was no different to any of the other days she'd stood on his front lawn, as if what they'd shared last night was nothing more than a cup of tea and a cookie between old friends. Man, if only he still felt that way about her. Everything was different now. He'd changed the rules of their agreement.

White shorts outlined her tan legs and a green top hugged her body, revealing the perfect plane of skin below her neck... He dragged the towel across the back of his shoulders.

Louis jumped from the doorway, struck a pose, and thrust out his tongue like a Māori warrior. "Is it okay if Jonty comes to pageant practice?"

Jonty raced back onto the deck, his hat sitting lopsided on his curls. Cy swallowed. "Ah, we're going... Sure. I guess we can come and watch. Give me a second to rinse off." He turned to walk up the steps.

"You don't need to come." Ellie's voice was light but distant. He turned back as she swung a bag over her shoulder. "It'll take a while today and I've got some sandwiches in here, so Jonty can stay with us for lunch. You take a break. I'll bring him back later."

All three of them stared at him and the tug-of-war inside reached breaking point. His body wanted more of her and his brain told him to back right off, just as she was doing.

He smiled at his son. "I'd prefer to come too, if that's all right. Are you okay with that, Jonty?"

His little boy nodded as he played with the scarf around his neck.

"Perhaps you boys could run along ahead then." He didn't need to tell them twice. The boys raced on, kicking up sand behind them.

Ellie pulled the sunglasses from her face. Her caramel eyes drew him in, but tiny lines dug into her forehead. "Is everything all right, Cy?" An uncertain smile traced her lips.

He folded his arms and looked up the beach at the boys. "Sure. Let's walk."

The skin between her eyes furrowed deeper, but she picked up her bag and started walking. "What's wrong? Is it about last night?"

Words scooted around his brain, and he fought to get them in the right order. He should probably do this face-to-face, but there was something soothing about walking beside her on the beach with the sun on his shoulders, looking straight ahead. "Yes. Last night." The words came out like speeding bullets. "I don't think we should let it happen again."

She stopped for a second, but then looked straight ahead and resumed walking.

"When I asked you to come into our lives, it was to help me show I had some stability in my life. What happened last night didn't feel stable. It felt wild and a bit out of control. That's not the way I want to feel right now. I shouldn't have made love to you."

"Then why did you?"

He stopped and waited while she turned. "Because I'm selfish. Just as I explained to you yesterday, I've always put myself first and if I keep doing that when Jonty needs me, I could lose him."

"I see."

"None of this is about you, Ellie. It's not that I regret what happened last night... God, I feel anything but regret. But I lay awake the rest of the night wondering if things are just too complicated between us now. That maybe Jonty and I should just leave. Before you and I get in any deeper, maybe I should take him back to the States and continue this fight on my own."

The perfect skin on her cheeks sagged the tiniest fraction. "You can't be serious. After all the progress Jonty has made here in the last two weeks, you'd consider walking away because you don't know how to deal with what happened between us last night?"

He turned his face away to the gently rolling waves. The strength in her tone galvanized him. "I don't want anything to jeopardize what we're going to do. All our energy has to be put into getting Jonty back. There's no space in my life for anything or anyone but him. Not now. Maybe not ever. I don't have room in my heart left for anything but my fight to be with my son."

"And in my deluded, optimistic world I thought you'd changed." A shadow crossed her face like a storm cloud across the sun.

"What do you mean?"

"I thought you'd learned some things about facing life's challenges, but I see I was wrong. You're prepared to use Jonty as an excuse for feelings you're too scared to look at and you'll hurt whomever you need to, Jonty included, to make that happen. It would be an enormous mistake to leave now."

She walked. The anger in her tone told him one thing. That he'd hurt her again. For a few moments of pleasure, he'd hurt her. They were silent for a moment, the only sound the scream of a seagull above them and Louis whooping up ahead. Was she right? Was he hurting Jonty, too?

She stopped and turned to face him again. "I told you right from the start that all I could offer you was a year of my life. I don't want anything from you in return, Cy, and if you think getting custody of Jonty will be compromised by a physical relationship with me, then there won't be one."

He stood there dumbfounded, and watched her walk

away. Part of him silently screamed in denial, despite this being what he'd asked for. That part of him wanted it all—Jonty being stable and emotionally healthy, full custody of his son, Ellie in his bed and in his life for good. But she was right. It was past time to stop being selfish and to do what he knew was right, despite the cost to himself.

"So, did you get some fresh air last night? Or at least the fresh bit?" Fleur faced the tumble of children onstage but a grin tugged at her mouth as Ellie turned beside her on one of the hard wooden seats in the hall.

A secret, sad heat curled through her as she looked down and dug a needle and thread into the ponga tree costume she was sewing for Jonty. Cy had gone back to the house to make some calls about the wedding, which meant Jonty could be involved in everything.

Fleur twisted to face her and lowered her voice. "When will you tell me what's going on between you and Cy? There's more to this engagement than meets the eye, isn't there?"

The needle pushed through the fabric into the flesh of Ellie's finger. "Ow!" She trapped the stinging spot in her mouth.

Fleur's eyes narrowed. "Good deflection, but not convincing." Her sister was silent for a minute as she took a mouthful of tea from the mug in her hands.

"He's going through a lot, with Jonty, the custody case." Ellie peered closer at a felt leaf she'd just finished creating.

"Something's happened, hasn't it?"

Broad silence hung between them before she turned to her sister. No more half-truths. "Is it that obvious?"

"If I hadn't been lying awake last night wondering what was taking you so long at Cy's, then the wide-eyed look you've been wearing all day would've given it away."

Ellie threw her fabulously intuitive sister her warmest smile. "I'm not wide-eyed. And it's complicated."

"Isn't it always?" Fleur huffed.

"No, this time it really is." Ellie smiled softly and stopped her sewing. "Cy and I slept together last night, but it won't be happening again."

"Really?" she asked.

Ellie pointed the needle and grinned. "I have weapons."

"How do you know it won't happen again?" She wriggled closer.

"Cy's very focused on Jonty right now, not our pretend engagement. He can't afford anything to unsettle what they're about to go through. He's having second thoughts about getting married." She forced breeziness into her voice, knowing these were Cy's words, but she didn't want her sister to worry.

"Doesn't that complicate things, though, having made a pass at him? It's going to be hard pretending for a whole year that it didn't happen."

"Cy was my first love. I won't deny it. And I got my heart broken. I won't deny that either. But I've moved on and..." She paused. "He was never in the same place as me, anyway. And I knew what I was doing last night. It's better that it happened now than when we're living together."

The children were called up onstage and they ran through the finale. Ellie couldn't drag her gaze away from the little boy with the golden curls moving to the center of the stage. His scarf was tied around his wrist as usual, and her heart swelled with joy.

"Gosh, that little boy's changed. Remember when he got

here and his head was always down and he shuffled his feet?" Fleur lifted the mug to her lips.

"Which is exactly why we can't let what happened last night happen again. There's too much at stake." Ellie laid the costume on her lap and turned to her sister. "Too many emotions tied up and they're bound to affect Jonty's progress."

"That's all fine and well, but last thing I remember, Cy walked out on you eight years ago and broke your heart. And I hope he hasn't just replayed his old tune. Jonty's emotions might be important, but so are yours."

"I was eighteen. Cy's right in that I needed space to focus on my own family back then, not him. I would've had my heart broken no matter who it had been. I know that now."

Fleur nodded. "But he was with you when William died." She laid her fingers on the bare skin of Ellie's arm. "Maybe this is what's happening here. You turning yourself inside out trying to save another little boy."

"It's not." Ellie covered her sister's hand with her own, her chin lifting. "Truly. I can help Jonty *and* Cy. By doing this one thing, something that doesn't cost me anything, I can avert this tragedy."

Fleur's gaze became more intense. "And if it's successful and Cy gets his son, what then?"

"Then after a reasonable amount of time—"

"You walk out of Jonty's life?"

Ellie sighed and nodded. "I know it's not ideal, but what other option is there? I'll be a friend to Jonty, so I'll go on seeing him, especially when they come back to the cove for holidays. Like an adopted aunt or something. I can see him as much as I see Louis. The break won't be sudden and it won't be permanent. And we can manage it with his therapist."

"And what about your feelings for Cy and his feelings for you?"

"If I keep my relationship with him as friends, it will guarantee I'm never out of Jonty's life. Imagine how completely devastating it would be if I started something with Cy and then it all fell to pieces. Then I'd never get to see Jonty again." She gripped the fabric harder. "And besides, I'm big enough to look after myself."

Ellie turned back to the stage to focus on the little boy at the center. It sounded hollow even in her own voice, but she wanted to make herself believe this as much as Fleur.

"I'm doing this for a friend who's done a lot for me and a little boy who deserves to be with his dad."

No matter what she said out loud, her inner voice spoke a completely different way. She did care. And she did possibly love him all over again...

10

———

"Crazy, useless..."

Ellie stood at Cy's back door the morning of the twenty-ninth, ready to knock. Curses followed by a roar of laughter made her hesitate. She hadn't seen him or Jonty much except for pickups and drop-offs for pageant practice. Cy was busy making wedding and flight plans, so he'd been happy for Ellie and Fleur to take Jonty. The distance hurt, but it was for the best. When they went into Auckland today to make more wedding arrangements, it would be as friends, the way Ellie wanted it to be from now on.

Cy's chuckle carried through the door. "What *is* this thing, Jonty? It looks like something from my Nana Doris' coal range. Like the ones they used in the olden days. I don't even know which way up it goes."

She knocked loudly and small feet drummed across the floor.

She grinned at Jonty as he peeked around the door. "Hi, I'm ready to go to Auckland to see Nana Pat." The smile he aimed back went straight to her heart. He wore nothing but jeans, his little bare-chested torso showing tan lines from his

148

T-shirt. And no scarf. She ruffled his hair as the significance of it burned like the sun in her chest.

She smiled at Jonty and pulled out the squishy bundle she'd been holding behind her back, and gave it to him. "This is for you."

His eyes grew huge as he stood staring at the bright blue-and-green toy pukeko bird. "I thought you might like to have a pukeko to take to America with you." She lowered her voice and leaned in to his ear, smelling sunshine and shampoo. "And you can use him when you're onstage."

Jonty's eyebrows shot up and he beamed.

"Hasn't he got lovely red legs and a beautiful red beak? When we take your chick to the sanctuary before we leave, we'll see lots of mum and dad pukekos that look just like that."

Jonty squeezed the toy tight, and her heart melted.

She stepped around a suitcase lying on the floor, clothes spilling from its corners. Jonty led her into the kitchen and the second she saw Cy, her pulse spiked. He leaned over a rickety-looking ironing board, an ancient iron in his hand and, if it were humanly possible, looked more handsome than she'd ever seen him before.

He looked up and his gaze danced over her, leaving a flush on her skin. "You look nice," he said.

"What, this old thing?" She grinned as she smoothed down the black cotton sundress that fitted tight around her waist and fell loose to her knees. "I haven't seen your mum in ages. I didn't want to wear my old shorts."

His eyes softened. "Are you worried about us telling her we're getting married?"

Ellie dragged her palm across her forehead and dropped her voice. "Do we really have to lie to her as well? Fleur knows the truth, and she won't tell anyone. Why don't we just be honest with your mum? I know she wouldn't tell anyone if she thought it would affect your chances of being with Jonty."

He lifted a shoulder and let it drop. "I know she wouldn't tell anyone, but it wouldn't be fair to her. She's in a well-known law firm in Auckland now and if they somehow found out she'd known about something that's potentially illegal, she could lose her job."

Ellie nodded. "Okay. I'll be glad when today's over though." She pointed to the iron. "What on earth is that?"

Cy rolled his eyes. "Good question. I wanted J to wear his best shirt for when he goes to visit his nana today. I washed it, but it looks a bit..."

He held up a bright orange shirt that could've been trampled by a herd of water buffalo. He shrugged. "I don't own an iron. And if I did, it wouldn't be one of these things. It looks like it's come from the Bronze Age."

Ellie winked at Jonty. "It's a very handsome shirt. I bet Nana Pat will love it."

Jonty reached into the suitcase, pulled out a T-shirt with a rocket on the front, and held it up. He looked at the orange mess Cy wrestled with and frowned.

"That's a good T-shirt, too," Cy said, "but it'll be nice to look your best for Nan." He grinned at his son, who shrugged and dropped the T-shirt back into the suitcase. "I'm gonna have to learn to iron your clothes for school anyway, J, so I'd better get it right."

Deep, hot pride flared inside her. Wanting to do things right, be a dad to his son in every way, was still new to Cy, and he was diving headlong into it. Over the course of these few short weeks, he'd become someone so new to her, so determined and focused, so loving and so giving, and it made her heart burst.

"Hey, look what you've got, J!" Cy said as Jonty squeezed the toy pukeko and it gave a squawk. Cy bent down as Jonty's mouth blossomed into a grin. "That sure was lovely of Ellie to give him to you." He smiled at her. "Thank you." The words wrapped softly around her heart.

"So, what are you up to here?" she asked, trying to regain her composure as she nodded at the ironing board. "I'd like to say I'd help, but that thing looks like it needs a license to drive it."

"Perseverance, that's the key." He stood and put the iron on the fabric. "Grab your toiletry bag, J. As soon as I finish this, we'll be off."

Jonty and his squawking toy trotted down the hallway and Ellie put her overnight bag on a chair. "What can I do to help?"

Tongue between lips and his focus on the shirt, Cy nodded toward the counter. "Could you tidy the breakfast things? I thought we'd have been ready earlier than this, but travel with a six-year-old isn't straightforward. Who knew you had to pack five toy cars, a terror sword, a skimboard, and a polished paua shell to show your nana?" He lifted his head and grinned. "Thanks again for the pukeko."

She busied herself with the breakfast things. "I thought that giving the real chick up might be tough on him."

"I hadn't thought of that."

"I almost bought one for myself, they're so cute." She put the peanut butter in the cupboard. "I bet your mum's excited about seeing Jonty."

Cy nodded. "I talked to her last night. She's over the moon. We'd agreed in the beginning that it was best to not overwhelm Jonty with too many people on this trip. But look how well he's responded to your family."

"He'll sure miss Louis when he goes back to the States."

So would she. But it would all be worth it for Cy to have his son with him always. They'd already set up Facetime and Zoom dates.

Cy tried to smooth the orange fabric under his hand. "I was thinking about that. Arrrgh!" He growled and flipped the shirt over. "What do you think Fleur would say if I flew her and Louis over at the end of next month? We'd be in the middle of the custody case, and it would be a great distraction for Jonty."

"They'd love it. I don't think Lou's ever been on a plane."

He sent her a smile and nodded. "It would be some company for you in the beginning. I could take Louis skiing, and I'm sure Fleur would love it."

She smiled at his thoughtfulness.

"And it would look great for the case. Having your sister and nephew there would make everything look more legitimate. As if we were really together."

Ellie steadied her hand on the counter. Of course, that was why he'd do it. For show, just as everything would be from now on. "It's a fabulous idea," she managed. "Can I be there when you ask Louis? He'll go nuts."

"Ow!" Cy stuck his thumb in his mouth and pulled back a foot as if ready to kick the board. "This is craziness. Maybe we should put Jonty in a T-shirt after all."

Jonty raced in with another armful of toys. It would be a shame if he didn't look his best for his nana. "Jonty, reckon you and I could give the ironing a whirl?"

He nodded emphatically as he looked at his dad.

Ellie took off her cardigan and rubbed her hands together. "Right, you go and get me some water in a jug and a little bowl, and we'll see what we can do." She stared down at the crumpled material. "I think I can remember how your great Nana Doris used to do it." She nodded at Cy. "You, Mr. Hathaway, can sit down and watch."

Cy rolled his eyes and grinned. He put the iron down and dragged up an old cane stool. "I don't think I've ever seen you undertake domestic duties, Ms. Jacobs. This should be good."

She screwed her face into a mock frown and her body relaxed. "Watch and weep at the iron maiden, Mr. Hathaway."

Jonty came back with the water, and she poured some into the iron and asked him to pour the rest into the bowl. He poked out his little pink tongue, screwed up his forehead, and completed the task without spilling a drop.

"Great job," she said, rubbing his back. "We'll put the iron up here out of the way while the steam gets started. Now, your Nana Doris used to have an old soda bottle with a little thing on top that sprinkled out water, but I don't think we'll find one of those. Let's try something else. I want you to put some water on your fingers like this." She dipped her fingers in the bowl and dripped water on the shirt.

Jonty's eyes widened, then slowly he copied. As soon as he was finished, a broad smile tracked across his face.

"It makes the shirt nice and damp, so it's easier to iron out the wrinkles." She let her gaze drift to Cy at the table. His stubbled chin was in his hands and he looked more relaxed than she'd ever seen him.

She put her fingers in the water, then turned and flicked them at Cy. "Hey!" he gasped, and his lips lifted in an indignant grin.

In the next moment, Jonty's hand shot into the bowl. He flicked water at his dad, his eyes as round as dinner plates. Cy lunged forward until his hand was in the bowl, and then he aimed first at Ellie, then Jonty. "So you think I'm all wrinkled, do you?"

"Right," Ellie yelled. "Come on, Jonty!" She raced into the kitchen, turned on the faucet, and she and Jonty flicked water at Cy.

Cy ducked and dived and grabbed at Jonty, then Ellie, his arm snaking around her waist before he drew her to him. Despite their closeness, Ellie squealed to be let go. Then she saw the glass of water that Cy lifted from the stainless-steel countertop.

"No. Cy, no!" The cool, fresh scent of him seeped into her and she weakened inside his strong hold. "This is the only nice thing I've got. Don't do it! Pleeeeeease!" Squirming, she giggled as the glass got higher and higher. Twisting around, she caught the wink Cy threw at his son as the first drops were about to spill over the lip of the glass.

Jonty jumped up and down, clapping his hands, his head bobbing. And then from out of his mouth, like church bells on a summer's day, came a belly laugh.

Cy stopped, frozen.

Ellie's heart swelled to bursting. Jonty looked at them, and then he laughed again. Ellie joined in, laughing so hard tears rolled down her cheeks.

She turned to Cy, and the look on his face undid her.

His eyes were liquid, his Adam's apple moving up and down. He shook his head, his hand still gripping the glass.

Instinctively, she curled her fingers around the hand he held rigid by his side. When he looked at her, it was like reaching into her own soul. Every muscle in his face moved with a different emotion—happiness, fear, relief, confusion. Everything passed across his features, and with each change, he squeezed her fingers tighter.

He let go of her hand, knelt down, and buried his head

in Jonty's curls. Ellie stepped back, the power of what she'd witnessed hovering around her like molten sunlight. Layer by layer, Cy was getting closer to his son. His beautiful little boy was healing. And minute by minute, she was starting to wonder if they really needed her anymore.

Quietly, she moved into the living room and picked up the steaming iron, the orange of Jonty's shirt swimming before her as she tried to squeeze away the tears. As she placed the hot steel onto the damp fabric, she hoped the hiss of steam would drown out the choking sobs that were boiling up from the deepest part of her. When had the minute rolled past—the second—that her connection to Cy changed from helping a friend to something that had the capacity to hijack her heart?

Later that morning, Ellie stood in the doorway of Cy's mother's house as Pat bent down and hugged her grandson. "I can't wait for you to show me everything you got for Christmas, sweetie," she said to her grandson, "but you'll be hungry after your drive, so go and see what I've laid out for your afternoon tea first." She gave him another squeeze. "Daddy told me you like the Tiny Teddy biscuits, so I got you some of those." Jonty threw his pukeko and terror sword on the nearest chair and headed for the kitchen.

"It's so lovely to see you, Pat." Ellie stepped into the open arms of Cy's mother and kissed her cheek. "It's been such a long time."

Pat hugged her close, then stood back to look at her, head tilted to the side. "When Cy called to tell me he was bringing you today, I still had an image of a skinny girl trying to outdo the boys at surfing." She grinned and her pale blue eyes sparkled. "He didn't mention what a beautiful woman you'd become."

Ellie sensed Cy move closer and when his hand snaked around her waist, all the blood in her body pooled beneath his touch.

"That's because I wanted you to see for yourself, and to see the way we feel about each other." Cy's voice was low as he reached down and laced his fingers with hers, then lifted her hand to his lips. "Mum, Ellie and I are getting married."

"Married?" Pat put a hand to her chest and her mouth fell open. "But I didn't even know you'd been back in touch with each other." She gave Cy a playful slap. "Cy, you're terrible. How could you have kept something so fabulous from me?"

He nestled into Ellie, and her knees weakened.

If this were real, she'd lean back into his strong chest, feeling supported and loved.

If this were real, she'd be used to the way the tiny hairs at the back of her neck stood up at his touch and the way her stomach flipped when he said her name.

If this were real, she'd let herself acknowledge the warmth threading through her body and the extra beat to her heart.

But this wasn't real. It was a lie that she was as much a part of as he was, and there was no changing it.

"We got back in touch when Ellie sent out the notices about the renovation, so it's all happened really quickly," Cy said. "What with having to get back to the States for the custody hearing, we decided to make the most of the couple of weeks at the cove, get married next week, then head back to Colorado together."

"Next week!" Pat shrieked. Her arm was on Ellie's now

and the looping in Ellie's stomach was turning into nausea. "We'll never organize a proper wedding in a week."

"It won't really be a proper wedding," Ellie said, and for the shortest second she wanted to tell this lovely woman that none of this was true, not the words, not the touching, none of it. She felt the warning as Cy squeezed her finger. "What I mean is," she continued, "we really need to get married so we can be together in the States, but we'd both love to have a proper wedding sometime, when the time is right." The lies flowed.

Pat smiled, satisfied. "Well, I just can't think of anything more wonderful," she said, her eyes glossy. "First loves finding each other after all these years." She touched Ellie's cheek. "And I couldn't think of a more perfect mother to my grandson."

Ellie swallowed past the lump in her throat.

"I don't have any bubbles, I'm afraid," Pat said as she wiped her eyes. "Sherry will have to do. You lovebirds take a seat while I check on Jonty, and then we'll toast your beautiful engagement."

When she was gone, Ellie slipped from Cy's touch and crumbled into the nearest seat, the dryness in her mouth making her voice catch. "That was terrible," she whispered.

"I know. I'm sorry." Cy took the seat opposite her and rubbed his thighs. His voice was low. "We had to do it, but it's over now. Mum's a realist, she'll understand when she finds out."

They sat in silence, listening to Pat chatting to Jonty about how lovely it would be having Ellie come back to the States with them.

"Telling Mum has proven one thing," Cy said. "She believed us totally. If anyone ever did ask if she believed our relationship was real, I'm sure she'd say yes."

Ellie nodded and sat back in her chair with a sigh. "That's why telling her the truth is going to be so hard."

Cy couldn't pull his gaze from Ellie as she pushed his son higher and higher in the swing. Her head was thrown back, hair shining golden in the midday sun, her tinkling laugh surrounding him like a cloak.

They'd accomplished everything they needed to in Auckland, including finding an engagement ring that was getting resized, but he couldn't wait to get back to the cove, even if their time was running out. The pressure of the lie they were about to embark on twisted his insides.

His mother had wished them well. She'd be at the wedding, of course, and she'd come over to support them through the custody hearing. She'd seemed so happy. If only they were getting married for real.

Cy leaned an elbow on the picnic table. He listened to Ellie chatting to his boy about all the things they'd seen in the city and what they might do when they got back to the beach.

For a minute, she stopped pushing and looked at Cy, a careful smile touching her face. Everything she'd done in the last two days had been careful, as if she were uncertain how he'd react. As she brushed hair from her cheek, he remembered the way her body had molded to his, the way she'd been confident enough to show him what she wanted when they'd made love.

He shook the memory and stood. He couldn't let Jonty sense any of his confusion. His son needed to believe his world was stable now. Unshakeable. That nothing, and no one, could cause him anxiety again.

As the swing slowed, Jonty dragged his feet on the ground, then jumped, and with his toy pukeko tucked firmly under his arm, ran to a slide on the opposite side of the playground. Still wearing the knitted sweater his nana had given him this morning for Christmas, he'd be sweltering in the summer sun.

"Come on, Cy," Ellie called as she took the empty swing, her back to him.

Hands in his pockets, he stayed where he was. Trying to forget how the silky hair falling in rivers down her back had felt against his chest.

"Come on. Give me a push at least."

He placed his palms on the bare skin where the fabric of her sundress dipped. Breathless desire tore through him. His fingers tingled with the touch and his senses filled with her flowery fragrance. He pushed her away, and she came swinging back, directly into his palms. Again, the fizz of closeness raced through him.

No matter how much he tried to bury this physical need for her, it wasn't working.

"Higher," she yelled. "I want to fly."

He stepped back and pushed her hard and her head tossed back, her hair softly grazing his arms as she swung away.

More and more he pushed, and each time she flew away, the desire in his limbs to be near her again grew with each touch.

He pushed her so high that the chains were almost parallel to the ground.

"Jonty!" she cried. "Jonty, look at me fly!"

From the top of the slide, Jonty waved at her, grinning widely.

They could be a family. Anyone driving by could look

and see a son playing on a slide, a father pushing a mother on a swing. But this picture wasn't real, and the lie sat bitter in his mouth. It was a distortion. A man who'd asked a woman to put her life on hold to help him, a woman who didn't want children but who'd sacrifice months of her career to be with a little boy because the man had nowhere else to turn.

He looked over to where Jonty pretended to give his toy pukeko a turn on the slide. He hadn't had a panic attack in four days, and for the first time in weeks, Cy felt that he was contributing to his son's progress, too. Being careful about each new experience, what he was exposed to and what he wasn't, was so important and would be for months to come.

"Swing with me," Ellie called to Cy. To stop himself from thinking, he folded himself into the swing beside her and pushed off.

As he swung higher with Ellie beside him and his son waving from the slide, he had the strangest sensation of being out of control, hurtling through space and being free. He let out a whoop and Ellie whooped back. Jonty came running from his slide waving his toy bird above his head.

"Do you remember?" Ellie asked, panting as her swing slowed. "When you built that tire swing out on the rocks by Leo's Point?"

He nodded. "And you were too scared to use it."

Tossing her head back, she groaned. "It was such a long way down. I watched you doing it day after day, telling me it would be all right, but it seemed so far. Such a risk."

Cy nodded, memories flooding him. "But you did it. One day you came with the rest of us. I remember the determined look on your face when you pushed to the front of the queue." His swing slowed, and he dragged his feet along the bark chips.

"I'll never forget how it took my breath away," she said. "The sense of accomplishment, of leaping out into the air, hoping I'd made the right decision that what you'd said was true and it would be all worth it in the end."

His swing had stopped and the chain links burned beneath his grip. He pushed his glasses on top of his head so he could see her better. "What made you do it? He concentrated on the light in her amber eyes and pushed out the question. "What changed your mind? After being scared so long, why did you decide to take the chance, get on that swing, and leap off into the sea?"

"Because I trusted you."

The steel of the swing chain heated beneath his grip. "Me?" The thump of the pulse in his throat almost buried the word.

She blinked. "I'd seen you build it and watched you jump off dozens of times. When you told me it was safe, that you'd look after me if I needed you, I believed you."

The chain links threatened to cut into Cy's fingers as he clenched them, a hundred-pound weight settling across his shoulders. If doubt had begun to crawl through his head since they'd made love, then this shot him between the eyes.

He'd meant what he'd said about no more sex, about keeping their distance for the sake of Jonty. And she believed him. Trusted him. But he didn't trust himself. The whole time they'd been in this playground, he'd imagined making love to her. She didn't want a long-term relationship, didn't want to be a wife or mother, and he was already asking her to put her career on hold.

The metal links burned beneath his hands. Words hadn't worked, actions hadn't worked. Someway, somehow he had to face the agony of his relationship with Ellie and solve this mess once and for all. It was the only way for them all to come out of this whole.

Back in Rata Cove the next morning Ellie sat in the hall putting the finishing touches to Jonty's tree costume for the dress rehearsal. The hall was hot as the sun beat through the high windows and the old overhead fans creaked in their effort to move the air around. Groups of kids waited for their turn to perform and parents sat around chatting.

Louis was out back getting into his *piupiu* skirt and having a *moko* drawn on his face for the *haka*. Over the past few days, the bigger boys had been working in secret on the special war dance with one of the Māori elders, and Ellie couldn't wait to see the pride on her nephew's face when they came onstage for the first time.

She lifted her head and watched Jonty playing with his iPad in the next row near some other boys. A smile pulled at her mouth as she saw the new toy pukeko tucked beside him on the bench. After he'd laughed yesterday, and the successful trip to Auckland and back, he seemed much more relaxed. She'd had to convince Cy to let her take the two boys on her own today, though, since Fleur was meeting up with some friends. In the end, Louis had told him it would be bad luck if too many people saw the *haka* before New Year's Eve, so Cy had reluctantly agreed, but he'd made Ellie promise to keep Jonty close.

"Jonty, come here, honey," she said, and he slid along his row and came to stand beside her.

"Let's try this on." She lifted the brown-felt construction over his head until his perfect little face poked through. His enormous blue eyes followed her movements as she rearranged the branches that were stuffed with newspaper and wire. When she sat back and looked at him, her throat closed. Tomorrow night he was going to stand onstage with a hall full of people watching, but he'd only have eyes for his daddy. She couldn't wait to see the look on Cy's face when he saw what his son had achieved.

"You look fantastic," she said, her voice wobbling as she pulled the costume back over his head and put it on the seat beside her. "When I've finished the bottom part, we can see how your toy pukeko fits in your arms."

"Ellie." Cyndi Rehua was holding up the hem of a sweet potato costume as the boy wearing it stood on tiptoes. "Would you mind putting a stitch or two in this so Jay doesn't keep falling flat on his face?"

"I'll be back in a minute," Ellie said to Jonty before she made her way to the stage. She was bent over, pins in her mouth and a needle dug into the cotton costume when a loud, guttural cry sounded from the side of the stage announcing the beginning of the *haka* and the ground began to beat with the thumping of feet. Each boy slapped his chest, then lifted his hands skyward, black-and-green swirls in rich *moko* patterns covering their faces. Their eyes were wide, and they alternately chanted and poked out their tongues.

She twisted to glimpse Jonty's reaction to such an incredible sight, and air seized in her chest. He wasn't in his seat. Just in time, she saw him through the window, running down the path. She stood and glided quickly through the group of children onstage, heart pounding, adrenaline flooding her body as she took the stairs two at a time. Damn, she should have anticipated this, should have told him what to expect. He'd probably never seen a haha before. Running out of the hall, the noise of the war dance behind her matched the terror racing through her blood. Where was he? Where would he go?

Arms pumping, body moving as quickly as she could make it, she arrived on the beach, the sand slowing her movements as she frantically searched. Where *was* he?

The road. The busy main road ran along the other side of the hall and holiday makers drove notoriously fast through the cove. If Jonty had gone out there...

"Ellie, is everything okay?"

She spun around to see Katie and some of the other girls, concern on their faces.

"Katie, Jonty's taken off. Please run down to Cy's house and let him know? If you other girls could come with me, we can spread out to look for him."

"On it," Katie said and ran down the sand.

"Could two of you cover the beach and two come with me to look on the roadside," Ellie said, a slow burn of panic digging into her chest.

By the time they'd made it to the road, some of the other parents had come out and were calling Jonty's name. Ellie raced from building to building, desperate for a glimpse of Cy's little boy.

Minutes passed and still there was no sign of him. Back at the hall, someone was talking about calling the community constable and one dad was texting around his friends for more people to come and search. While Ellie was giving a description of what Jonty was wearing, Cy came running up from the beach.

She left the group and ran to meet him. "He was frightened by the boys doing the *haka*. He hadn't seen it before and I should've talked to him about—"

Cy's blazing eyes looked everywhere but at her. "It

doesn't matter what happened. It matters where he is. Which way did he go?"

He put his hands above his eyes to shield the glare of the sun and twisted around.

"I'm not sure. I didn't see..."

He stopped turning, then faced her. "He wasn't with you?"

"Yes, he was with me, but he moved so quickly. I didn't—"

He held his arms out in a desperate gesture. "He's six, Ellie. If you'd run straight after him, you must've seen which way he went."

Had she run straight after him, or had she been so shocked by what happened she'd waited a second too long?

"Cy, I'm sorry, I don't—"

"There's no time for sorry, Ellie," he said, his voice sharp and cold. "We just need to find my boy."

11

Cy left Ellie standing outside the hall and sprinted up the driveway to the road.

Tears, hot and sharp, stung at the back of Ellie's nose, but she swallowed them away and swiped her hand across her eyes. That wasn't going to do Jonty any good, and Cy's reaction was understandable. If she'd warned Jonty what to expect, explained what the chanting and the slapping of chests meant, then he wouldn't have taken such fright. If Cy had been to the practices has he wanted, he'd have prepared Jonty.

"Aunt Ellie!" Louis came running up to her, tattoos still covering his face, the long flax beads on his *piupiu* skirt chattering as he ran. "Someone said Jonty's gone, that he was scared of our *haka* and the *moko*."

Louis's eyes were bright and Ellie laid a hand on his shoulder. "Do you have any idea where he'll be, Lou? It's really important that we find him quickly."

Louis twisted and looked back toward the beach. "There's a driftwood pile near Starfish that we found last night. You can crawl in the middle of it like a hut. He could be there."

"Show me," she said.

Minutes later, they drew up near a pile of driftwood. Louis ran the last few steps, knelt down and looked in, and gave her the thumbs-up. A wave of relief crashed over her, Ellie thought her heart would stop beating. Steadying herself, she swallowed past the lump in her throat and let out a small sob.

"Hey, J," Louis was saying. "It's me, look. We have to wear these for the *haka* and we do all that chanting to send the bad things away and tell everyone how tough we are. We're not the real warriors, this is just makeup like Ellie wears sometimes." He dragged his hand across his cheek so that the elaborate design was smudged.

There was no sound from the driftwood pile, but Louis continued. "You can't be scared of this, J, because we'll be doing it onstage with you tomorrow night. If your dad thinks you're too scared to be with all of us, then he's not going to let you come tomorrow and you won't be able to give him your surprise. The fie nally won't be the same if you're not in it with your pukeko, J. Won't you come back to the hall?"

Louis's head dropped, and he stood and brushed the sand from his skirt. Ellie's heart squeezed for her beautiful nephew and all he'd done for Jonty. Turning back to Ellie, he shrugged, the look of defeat on his face heart breaking.

He walked back toward her when a piece of driftwood was pushed aside and Jonty peered out.

Don't run to him. Cy's voice from the very first time she'd met Jonty played in her head. *It'll just make it worse.* "Hey, Jonty," she said quietly. "We're so happy to have found you."

He crawled out from the wood and gave a watery smile.

"You'll explain it all to Cy, won't you Ellie?" Louis said in a rush. "I was just a bit scared, that's all, but we have to make sure Cy lets him come tomorrow, and that it's still a surprise, or everything will be ruined."

The weight in Ellie's chest suggested there could be a lot more ruined than just Jonty's dream of surprising his father onstage. The way Cy had looked at her, the way he'd blamed her for not paying enough attention to his son, made her heart shrivel.

"I'll do what I can," she said. "What we need to do right now is get Jonty back to his dad."

When they reached the beach, Cy looked up from where he was speaking to a group of men. Seeing the way his body slackened in relief at the sight of his son brought tears to her eyes.

Jonty's hand dropped from hers and he raced forward, Cy opening his arms before Jonty hit his father's embrace like a bullet. Cy kneeled and buried his face in his son's hair.

Louis spoke in the background. "He's okay, Cy, he just got scared by our costumes for the *haka* but now he's seen us he wants to come back in and watch, don't you Jonty?"

The boy looked up at his father and then over at his friend and nodded.

Cy shook his head and squeezed his son tightly. "I think that's enough excitement for one day. I'm sure Ellie will watch you, Lou."

"Cy, could I have a quick word?"

"Maybe later. I'd like to take Jonty somewhere quiet." He stood and lifted Jonty onto his hip.

Louis's voice was hollow and small beside him. "Jonty'll miss the practice if he goes home now."

Cy turned to Ellie's nephew. "I'm sorry, Lou. J's had a big

fright. I'll take him home for a rest and we might see you later."

He turned toward home, but Ellie put a hand on his shoulder. "Cy, wait. It wasn't as bad as you think."

His voice was tight and controlled. "Thanks for finding him."

"Please, can we talk?" She headed up the beach and motioned for him to join her.

He placed Jonty back on the sand and followed.

"Please don't make this into a bigger deal than it is." Her hair blew across her lips and she swiped it away with a finger. "It was just a fright; that's all."

He ripped the sunglasses from his face and glared at her. "Just a fright? God, Ellie, he could have been hit by a car or swept away by a wave. I told you I didn't want him pushed. I explained what the consequences could be, but you didn't listen."

"He was just taken by surprise. It could've happened to anyone who hadn't seen a *haka* before. I was busy helping with costumes and—"

"Couldn't you have held his hand? Explained what was going on?" The tone of his voice made the words feel like bullets . "Taken him out when it started, so he wasn't frightened and alone?" She watched his chest rise and fall, and then he spoke more quietly. "But it's not your fault, it's mine. I should have been there. I should have been at the hall. He took a step toward her and a soft, sympathetic look crossed his face. I don't know, Ellie, maybe you've been right all along and I've just refused to accept it. What I've asked you to do is too much. This whole plan has been a mistake."

Ellie's heart stuttered and her blood froze in her veins. The ground rushed toward her as Cy turned and began walking up the beach.

~

"Don't you dare walk away from me."

A band squeezed around Cy's throat as he turned to see Ellie kneeling on the sand. "Ellie, each time Jonty has had a panic attack in the last two weeks, it's because I've let myself become distracted. I don't know what I was thinking, asking you to marry me and come back with us. Jonty and I will be packing and leaving for the States tomorrow."

She rose unsteadily to her feet. "You're leaving? You selfish bastard." She sucked in a breath, then met his gaze again, daggers flashing in her eyes. "And there he is again, the Cy I'd *so* hoped was gone forever. The one who can't stand strong when times get tough, the one who runs away so he doesn't have to face the people who care about him. Admit it, this isn't about Jonty at all. It's about *you* and what makes you frightened."

His chest squeezed tight, trapping air in his lungs.

She stepped forward and set her hands low on her hips. "I know he had a setback today, but whenever that happens, he always comes back fighting and takes two steps forward the next day. You asked me to help fight for Jonty, and that's exactly what I'm going to do. Starting right now. You want to run away again, fine, but don't you *dare* use that little boy as an excuse to justify your behavior."

His body vibrated with tension. He wanted to tell her the truth. She was doing this because she cared, even though it was costing her and he owed it to her to let it all out. He lowered his voice as his gaze swung to where the boys were playing in the distance and back again. "You're right, Ellie, I am frightened. I left you all those years ago to protect you, and I need to do it again. Don't you see? I have to walk away because I know you're going to end up hurt again. I thought

I could keep your heart safe, but I don't know how to be with you without hurting you."

"Give me one more day," she whispered. "One more day to prove to you we can make this work."

God, if it were only that simple. He scrubbed his hands over his face. Things had gone too far. Too many hearts were on the line here, his attraction to her too strong. *And yet*, a little voice in his head whispered, *what if?*

What if Ellie was right? What if he *was* running when he didn't need to? Cy looked over to where his son stood with Louis, then back to Ellie *What if?* He studied the hopeful expression in her eyes and his resistance crumbled.

"Okay." He nodded. "One more day."

Gwin: *So sorry girls, I can't talk long tonight. I'm in the middle of a family drama, but I wanted to see how things are going, Ellie.*

Ellie: *Is everyone okay? Is it your mom? Your niece?*

Gwin: *Everyone's still breathing at the moment, but when I get my mom in a room by herself, I mightn't be responsible for my actions. Let's just say cat amongst pigeons, bulls in china shops, they ain't got nothing on my mom and her ability to screw everyone up.*

Kirin: *Hope it's not going to alter your plans for moving, Gwin?*

Gwin: *I'm not sure how that's going to go. Someone from our past has turned up unexpectedly, and it could put everything on hold, but I'll keep you posted. Enough about me, though. What's happening with you, Ellie?*

. . .

Ellie told them what had happened. About the terror she'd felt when she realized Jonty wasn't in the hall, the frantic, desperate search for him, and the overwhelming relief when Louis had found him.

Kirin: *Bless that nephew of yours. Sounds like he and Jonty have been really in tune this whole time.*

Gwin: *Cy must have been so grateful when Jonty was found.*

Ellie: *He **was** grateful, but he's changed his mind about everything.*

Kirin: *What do you mean everything?*

Ellie: *Getting married. Me coming to the States. Using me to help with the custody battle.*

Gwin: *What the hell? What brought this on?*

Ellie: *Cy thinking that his feelings for me are causing him to lose focus on his son. That if he hadn't been so distracted, Jonty would never have gone missing.*

Kirin: *Oh, for God's sake. I know Cy's been through a lot, but now's the time for him to be strong for all of you, not to give in when something goes wrong.*

Ellie: *Running when things get tough is Cy's default position. It's like when the emotions get too deep, he doesn't know how to deal with them, so he runs.*

Gwin: *I'd say you've hit the nail directly on its head.*

Ellie: *I'd been hoping that was just the old Cy, that he'd grown and changed. I know it comes from a place of fear—the way he felt when his parents used to fight. He'd come over to our place and pretend it wasn't happening, but I know it affected him deeply. I want to help him see that, to show him that he can stand up for what he wants.*

Kirin: *Maybe it's his feelings for you that scare him.*

Ellie: *The thing is, I know he has strong feelings for me. I feel* *it when he touches me, in the way he looks at me. If I'm honest, I feel as though we've gone past a point of no return. Jonty's bonded with me too, and cutting me out now's going to leave everything in a bigger mess. Which is why I've asked him to give me one more day.*

Gwin: *One more day for what?*

Ellie: *For me to prove to him that I can help him gain custody, that I am good for Jonty and that we can resist the pull of each other for the greater good. Jonty and Louis have something planned for tomorrow night and I'm really hoping it turns out well, for all our sakes.*

Ellie's fingers hovered in the air above her keyboard, waiting for Gwin and Kirin to tell her she was crazy, that she was holding onto something that was only going to hurt her. There was a distinct pause, and then three dots illuminated beside both their names, indicating they were replying.

Kirin: *Good for you. You've stayed true to your loving heart, Ellie. No matter what happens now, you have to know that you've put it all on the table for Cy and his little boy.*

Gwin: *Just what I was going to say. You've put yourself on the line this whole time, Ellie. No matter how things turn out tomorrow, you have to know that's true.*

Ellie: *I know it. But I also know if Cy does what he says he'll do and leaves without me, I don't know if my heart will stand it.*

Kirin: *But you've done it once before. The last time Cy walked away from you, you picked yourself up; you got on with your life and you made a huge success of it. Everything you've done at the cove has been for other people and I really hope Cy can see that. But most of all, I hope he chooses you.*

Gwin: *Please check back in with us tomorrow if you need to.*

Ellie: *We'll be thinking of you too, Gwin. Fingers crossed everything works out for your family.*

Gwin: *As I said, the holidays make people crazy. Good luck for tomorrow, Ellie.*

Ellie: *Thanks, I'm going to need it.*

~

A rainbow of T-shirts and shorts, sarongs, and tank tops drifted through the sticky dusk air and into the Rata Cove Memorial hall for the New Year's Eve pageant the following evening. Groups of teenagers stood around a stack of driftwood set on the beach for the bonfire celebrations at midnight.

Cy thrust his hands in his pockets and climbed the stairs, smiling at neighbors and greeting people he hadn't seen for years. But a yawning emptiness expanded inside him. This was all about to end. Old black-and-white photos of the cove were dotted in collages around the walls, dredging up memories that made what he had to do that much more difficult.

He'd be leaving here tomorrow, and the simplicity, the beauty of life at the beach would be over. A new phase would begin. He'd focus on Jonty from now on—and while that was exciting, too, he was going to miss Rata Cove and all it had given him. Above all else, the emptiness in his chest was because he'd be leaving here without Ellie.

After agreeing to wait one more day, he'd half expected her to come by early and try to talk him out of his plan to leave, but he hadn't seen her until late in the afternoon. She'd dropped by asking if Jonty could help Louis with something for the pageant, and Jonty had been out the door before Cy could reply. It seemed she'd come to the same realization he had. For Jonty's sake, and for Ellie to live the life she really wanted here in New Zealand, a relationship between them—imaginary or otherwise—was impossible.

He scanned the crowd for his son's mop of blond curls, but he couldn't see anyone. Not Jonty, not Fleur, not Ellie.

"Hi, Mr. Hathaway." Katie Newport handed him a bright green program, and he put a gold coin in her tin.

"Hey, Katie. The hall looks great. Did you decorate it?"

Her face flushed as she nodded. "Mum said we should celebrate Ellie bringing the cove back to life, so we found old photos to remind people of everything that's happened here in the past."

"You've done a great job." Pride for Ellie's efforts swelled in his chest, side by side with longing.

He chose a seat right at the back and the lights dimmed before he'd even sat down. People chatted and moved about, the ice cream and toffee apple trolley doing a roaring trade. He kept an eye trained on the door for any sign of Jonty and Ellie, a clutch of nerves buried inside him. He pulled out his phone to text her.

"Mind if I sit here?" Fleur stood beside him, flushed and disheveled. "It's like a mosh pit back there." She flicked her hair over her shoulder and grinned. "So much for a summer holiday!"

"Have a seat."

"Jonty's with Ellie. I hope that's all right."

He put the phone back in his pocket and brushed a hand across his chin. "For the whole show?"

Fleur grinned as she settled into her chair. "Yeah, for most of it."

He craned his head to see where they were sitting, if there was a spare seat nearby.

"Oh, they're not in the audience," Fleur said. "They're out back."

Of course. Jonty wanted to be with Louis for the pageant. It would be the last time they'd be together. It couldn't be helped. But what would happen to Jonty and Louis's friendship when they weren't part of each other's lives anymore?

He settled into his seat, relaxing as the curtain creaked open.

It was a great show, with the same songs kids in this part of the world had sung for thirty years. Māori songs and *poi* dances, little skits about things that went on at the beach, even a poem that some of the girls had written about Ellie being the princess who'd brought the town back to life.

The show continued on, and his heart grew heavier. Louis came onstage stuttering lines several times and Fleur mouthed along with him. Once, when Louis stood frozen, head darting about for help, Fleur stood and called his line in a hoarse whisper and people giggled around them. Louis threw his mum a look of simple love.

After an hour, the red velvet curtains closed, and enthusiastic clapping was almost drowned out by the thundering of feet backstage. Then silence fell, punctuated by the odd hiss of, "*Shhhh!*" from the stage. Callum was two rows in front and had a camcorder lifted to his eyes.

"The finale was always spectacular." Betty Browning leaned over and put a hand on his arm.

"Remember when you used to be in the finale, Cy? That year you came riding in on Bill Hanson's old Clydesdale nearly gave Mrs. Butterthwaite a heart attack."

Cy grinned and patted her hand. A hush fell over the audience as the static from the PA indicated music was about to start for the finale. Anxious parents leaned forward in their seats and little brothers and sisters wriggled in anticipation of the supper afterward.

The squeak of the curtain put the final silence on the voices around him. Lights came on, green and brown, and Cy stared as a lone figure was revealed at the center of the stage. It was someone dressed as a tree—a short and straggly sort of tree—with a hole cut for the face.

His chest hollowed, and the air died in his lungs. It wasn't...was it? He leaned forward, his fingers curling around the edge of his chipped wooden seat. Like a bass drum, his heart beat deep in his throat. There was no mistaking the wideness of those eyes, or the golden curls that peeped from under the leaf-lined headpiece. His lip trembled, and he squeezed his eyes shut before opening them again.

It was his boy. Jonty Hathaway stood on a stage, thousands of miles from home with no one beside him. A bolt of electricity fired through Cy's limbs and he shot out of his chair. The silence was broken by people twisting in their seats, shuffling to look at him.

He stared at the stage. What if Jonty was frightened? What if he panicked and no one was there to rescue him?

A smile as big as the Atlantic covered his son's face as the recorded strains of children singing echoed around the room. "On the first day of Christmas my true love gave to me, a pukeko in a ponga tree."

Lifting his little arms, Jonty revealed a nest in his fern-like hands and inside was his toy pukeko, its bright red legs stuck out the side. A collective sigh went up from the audience and necks craned to get a better look. Blistering pride filled Cy. Despite everything he'd been through, his son was fighting to find his voice. Find his place in the world.

Hands touched Cy from both sides, guiding him back

into his seat. His nose stung with the effort to keep emotion in, but he continued staring, frightened he'd miss something. When had his son learned all this? When had Jonty found the courage to be on his own and mouthing the words to a crazy Christmas song?

Children's voices sang with gusto over the sound system. "On the second day of Christmas my true love gave to me, two kumara and a pukeko in a ponga tree". Two purple sweet potatoes waddled on to stand beside Jonty, but Cy couldn't keep his gaze from his incredible little man. His son turned in a ponga-tree pirouette and the audience murmured their approval.

"Isn't he fantastic?" Fleur whispered. "Look at the little toy pukeko there. Can you believe it? It was all Ellie and Jonty's idea. She sewed his costume. They've been working on it for over a week. They wanted to surprise you."

Cy couldn't stop the fat, salty tear that squeezed from his eye and tripped on his cheek.

A miracle had happened. Something incredible had been going on for days and he'd been blind to it. All the hope that he'd kept locked down threatened to boil over. How could he ever take Jonty away from here?

"On the third day of Christmas, my true love gave to me..." Jonty looked to the side of the stage and a trio of flax baskets came waltzing on. But something else caught Cy's eye, and he rubbed a hand across his face to clear his vision. Sitting just offstage in the shadows, but with her distinctive blonde hair tumbling around her shoulders, was Ellie, clapping. Understanding punched Cy like a hundred-pound weight, and his heart seized in his chest.

She did this for Jonty.

He rubbed his cheek with the back of his hand as Ellie gave Jonty the thumbs-up. His attention darted back to his son singing the next line with the other children. "On the fourth day of Christmas, my true love gave to me…"

His chest pounded, and a new sensation caused his heart to swell. He loved Ellie Jacobs. For her selflessness, her willingness to fight so hard for what was good. He loved her because she made him believe he could do what was right, but would challenge him when he wasn't. Most of all, he loved her for her beautiful, trusting heart and the way she opened it to everyone around her. Including him. He loved Ellie Jacobs, just as he'd feared he would. He loved her and couldn't bear the thought of living without her.

She'd been prepared to do everything he asked, cross the world to help him win his little boy while her own dreams slipped away, and he'd done nothing but think of himself. Even when he'd tried to run because things got too intense between them, she'd made this happen for his son.

Tears streamed down his face as his shy little boy stood in front of hundreds of people, head held high, lips moving in song. Jonty was healing. All because of Ellie. She'd done for his son what he'd been unable to do for himself all these years. Now he had to give Ellie something *she* really wanted. He only hoped it wasn't all way too late.

Ellie sat transfixed. She'd hoped and prayed that Jonty could carry this through. To see him standing in front of all those people, a smile blossoming on his face because his father was watching, was incredible.

He danced with the sweet potatoes and the flax baskets, and every now and then he'd look out into the audience and grin even wider.

She followed his gaze out to where Cy sat like a statue in

the crowd. Spellbound. Light from the stage reflected on his sandy hair and his glowing face. Her heart grew so huge, she thought it would burst. This sweet little boy had slipped under her skin and sailed straight into her heart. Her bottom lip wobbled but she trapped it between her teeth and pulled her shoulders back. This was Jonty's and Cy's moment; it had nothing to do with her.

So why did her eyes sting and why was her throat closing over? She forced a smile and drew in ragged air.

Because I love Jonty.

The thought sliced through her. She blinked to keep focused on the stage. She loved him. *This wasn't supposed to happen.* Seven eels pushed their way past her and wriggled around Jonty. He mouthed the words along with the rest of the children and swayed his ponga-tree arms. Her heart beat hard. How proud Cy must be of his darling little boy. She turned to look for him again, but his empty chair caused her pulse to dip.

There he was. He'd moved closer and was rubbing the sleeve of his jacket across his eyes. How she wished she could be beside him, slip her hand in his and share this incredible moment together.

The feeling cut into her. All the questions, the doubts, the indecision of the last week surged within her and climaxed in one pure and simple truth.

She loved Cy.

Sucking in a breath, her heart swelled. Of course, she loved Cy. She always had. But when you'd lived with this ache for so long, pushed it away, tried to shape it into something else—it was hard to recognize what was left. But it was love. Almost the same as it had always been, but now with a fierce desire, a burning need for him that took her breath away. A mature love about deep understanding and even deeper acceptance. Little by little, truth squeezed past the armor of denial she'd been wearing.

Her fingers twined in her lap, and she knotted them together. He'd wanted her as his plastic wife, a stand-in mother, and now he was leaving her again because it had all got too hard. Every cell in Ellie's body screamed at her to run—to get away and let out the choking sob welling from deep inside. But her feet were bolted to the floor, vision hooked by a little boy in a tree costume. Nothing good came from running. She wished with all her heart that Cy knew that.

She *had* to go through with the marriage. For Cy and his remarkable little boy to be together..

Louis took the stage with ten other boys doing the *haka*, their feet stamping in unison on the polished wooden floor. Jonty turned and watched his buddy, no sign of panic on his face, and Ellie was so proud of the two of them.

Finally, as twelve girls in reed skirts joined the throng onstage, Ellie's gaze was drawn to Cy, and she bit her lip at the smile that lit his face. He'd be so excited, so relieved, and so ready to go back to the States and show what he and Jonty had achieved in New Zealand.

When the final curtain dropped, Jonty came running to her, his golden curls bouncing as he pulled off his headdress.

"Oh, sweetie, you were incredible." Kissing his soft cheek, she breathed in his scent of soap and shampoo. "You were amazing," she whispered, letting backed-up tears fall. "Wonderful. Listen to all those people still clapping for you."

With his toy bird tucked under his branch arms, Jonty pulled aside the red velvet curtain and peeked out, which caused chuckles and more applause from the audience.

When he looked back at her his tiny white teeth flashed as his face broke into a grin.

While dozens of children churned around them, she pulled him close again. He wrapped his little arms around her and squeezed tight.

"Jonty." The deep voice behind her was unmistakable, and Ellie stayed rooted to the spot. She kept her misted gaze on the boy locked in her arms. If she looked at Cy, she'd unravel.

Jonty bolted into his father's arms. The stubby branches and green felt leaves stuck into every part of Cy's body. His father's head shook and his lips moved at his son's ear.

"Wow, you were so cool, dude!" A bare-chested Louis, with his *piupiu* and painted face, slapped Jonty on the back. "Is Jonty allowed to come out back and have supper with us, Cy?"

Jonty turned to his father, and Cy nodded. "Of course he can." His voice dipped, then righted itself. "I'll be there in a minute."

As the boys ran off, Ellie bent to pick up discarded song sheets. She brushed away tears.

"Ellie." Cy's voice was low, and she fumbled with the latch of her bag. He placed his hand on the bare skin of her arm. "I had no idea you were doing this with Jonty. It's incredible."

She lifted her bag and smoothed her hair over her shoulder. Unable to stifle the pride in her own heart, she smiled at him. "Wasn't he fantastic? It was all his idea. None of us coaxed him into it." His touch called her, drew her in, but she reminded herself that this moment was about Cy and his son, not the secret whirl of emotion raging through her.

Stitching a smile to her face, she stepped back. He was

going to tell her it wasn't enough. That despite everything he'd just witnessed, they'd be leaving here without her.

"God, Ellie, what can I say but thank you. For everything you've done for Jonty." His voice splintered. "Do you *know* what that meant to me? Seeing him so independent? So confident? So happy?"

His tone, the way he looked at her... Her heart slammed against her breastbone and all she could utter was a choking sob. "Oh, Cy, it's going to be so hard."

"What is, Ell?" His voice husky.

Her throat constricted and tears ran down her cheek. "Everything." She dredged a breath. "It's going to be so hard saying goodbye." Her hand shook as she swiped hair off her face.

He pulled away slightly, then lifted her chin. "Have you changed your mind?"

Of course not, her heart screamed. *I love you. You, who needs my name on a marriage license. You, who sees me as a dependable friend. You, who makes love to me like your life depends on it but can offer me nothing more.*

She hiccupped as she forced the tears down and blew out a breath. "I haven't changed my mind. I thought that after yesterday you didn't want me to come, but I so wanted you to see that with a little time, things can feel good again."

He reached for her hand and gave it a squeeze. "And I'm so glad you made me stay. I wouldn't have missed this for the world. I can never thank you enough."

Her lungs screamed and she realized been holding her breath. She had a question to ask and whichever way Cy answered, she knew his reply would devastate her. "You think I can still help you?"

He put a hand on her shoulder and pinned her with his

gaze. "Of course I do. I want you to be part of everything now, Ellie. I want to be with you"

He said how he was so sorry that he'd erupted when Jonty ran out, but she hardly heard any of it. While she'd been having her epiphany about how much she loved Cy Hathaway and his son, Cy had been rejoicing in the belief that his plan was finally coming together. He might still want her to come with them, but his feelings for her hadn't changed.

Callum Brown walked by with his son and Cy touched her arm. "Ellie, I need to do something really quickly. When I get back, we'll go to supper and have the best New Year's Eve ever." He excused himself, called out to Callum, and went to talk with his old friend.

As Ellie watched them talking together in the wings, she finally let backed-up tears fall. Tonight had been everything she'd hoped for Jonty. Seeing him with his little chest thrust out so full of self-confidence, the shining glow of pride when he'd come on the stage—it was everything he and Cy deserved, and more. But what had it done for her? It had made her realize that despite everything, she still loved Cy. For the way he loved his friends and family, for the way he could challenge her and make her question some of the tough things she'd believed about herself for so long—like whether she had what it took to love and care as a mother. The way he knew her like no one else ever would. The way she felt in his arms.

Yes, tonight had changed everything in Jonty's world, and Cy's, but it had left her with the realization that one year from now, they'd be moving on with their lives and she'd be losing Cy all over again.

12

Late afternoon on January the third, Ellie stood in front of a projector screen in the memorial hall showing the townsfolk for the last time the amazing changes they'd see in the coming year. There'd be a fresh new look to everything, brand-new buildings and renovations for the old. Her mind, however, was fixed on where she'd be tomorrow—standing in a registry office with a ring that meant nothing and a marriage license that meant even less.

She, Cy, and Jonty had seen the new year in together, then walked back home a little after midnight, Jonty asleep in Cy's arms. Cy had continued to thank her over and over, but when they parted at his holiday house, she'd felt bereft all over again.

The last two days had gone by in a whirl. Cy had been busy on the phone much of that time, making wedding and travel arrangements, and today he and Jonty had taken the pukeko chick to the sanctuary. They'd said they'd come and tell her how it went but she hadn't seen any sign of them.

Yesterday had been her last full day with Louis and

Fleur. This afternoon they'd gone into Papaatawhai to meet some friends and they'd arranged to come to the hall when she'd finished and walk back up the beach together one more time.

She clicked to the next slide and everyone exclaimed at her design for renovations to the hall. There'd be a new kitchen with a caterer's oven to replace the one with the single element and the two temperatures—frozen and incinerator—as well as a bigger backstage area for shows and pageants. She looked out to the sea of smiling faces and realized that this place was part of her heart and she was going to miss it so much.

She felt the warmth of the people around her, the joy that their town was coming back to life, but her blood ran cold. Cy was sticking to his word. No more touching, no more getting close. Since they'd slept together, everything had changed, and now that Jonty was on the way to a recovery, Cy might not even need her for the whole year. But wasn't this what she'd always wanted? For Jonty and his dad to be growing closer, for Cy to gain confidence in being a dad, and for her to have the time and space to go back to her business?

A headache bit deep behind her eyes and the strain of tears that begged release threatened. She swiped a hand across her face, drew in a sharp breath, and flicked to the next slide. Tomorrow they'd travel to Auckland to get married and then they'd fly off to the States, another day closer to when she'd finally say goodbye to Cy and Jonty forever.

"Ellie." Her name called from the back caused the hall full of people to swivel in their seats. Cy stood at the door, just as he had two weeks ago, before she'd let him steal her heart. He wore a tight-fitting black T-shirt over faded jeans, his signature aviators hooked in the front. A smile glowed on his face.

"Cy," she said. "I won't be long."

He strolled forward, one hand in a pocket as Fleur, Louis, and Jonty moved in behind him and took a seat in one of the back rows.

"Ellie, there's something I need to tell you."

The intensity of his tone nearly stopped her heart. *This is it.* He'd realized that with all Jonty's progress, with the complicated relationship between them, he didn't need her anymore. Her temples tightened, and she put her hands behind her back so he couldn't see them shaking.

And he was doing in here. In public.

He took a step forward. "Ellie, everything's changed."

"No, you're wrong," she said, not caring that half the town was hearing this conversation. It didn't matter who saw that she loved Cy now. "Nothing's changed. Tomorrow we get married and move to the States."

Cy reached into his pocket and pulled out his phone. "Before you say anything else. I'd like to show you, and everyone here, something."

Ellie waited while he fiddled with his phone and then her laptop propped on a table. When he finally stood back, the chorus of "A Pukeko in a Ponga Tree" streamed out of the hall speakers and a close-up of Jonty filled the screen. Despite her anguish, a smile pulled at her mouth and she chuckled. He looked even more amazing from the audience view. He'd been so brave, so gorgeous and so courageous.

She turned to Cy and frowned. "I don't understand. Why are you showing us this now?"

He turned the sound down, but still the images of the New Year's Eve pageant played on the enormous screen. "Callum sent me the video clip of Jonty singing and I sent it to Maria and Jeff, Susan's parents. Yesterday I called them and we had a really long talk. They can't believe the progress Jonty's made in only two weeks. They've dropped the custody case."

"Oh, Cy!" Ellie pressed fingers to her lips. "No wonder his face had been shining when he'd arrived here. This was the most incredible news. And the most devastating. If Cy didn't need her for the custody case, then he was leaving here without her.

She straightened and moved to the edge of the stage, her hands across her stomach, acid rising in her throat.

Cy walked up the aisle between the rows, then up the steps and onto the stage until he was only a few feet from her. "I came here today to tell everyone the truth, because everyone's been affected by what I asked you to do." He threw an arm wide. "I need everyone in this hall, everyone in this whole town, to know what an ass I've been in these last two weeks. I've been selfish. I've only thought about what I need, and I've lied to all of them. Now's the time to tell them the truth."

"Please don't do this," she whispered.

He took two steps toward her, but turned toward the audience and addressed them. "Two weeks ago I came back to the cove to ask Ellie to be my wife to help win custody of my son."

A communal gasp went up and Ellie steeled herself.

"Why did I come all the way back here to ask Ellie?" He turned to look at her again, his face filled with intensity and passion. "Because she has the kindest, most generous heart of anyone I've known. You all know how true that is, don't you? Ellie's the one you bring a sick bird to because she's so smart and so gentle. She's the one who can pull a broken community back together like she's done for this town, and do it all for free." Another gasp went up as people turned to each other.

If only the old wooden boards of this stage would open up and swallow her whole. She knitted her hands together to stop them trembling and waited for the sucker punch when he'd tell her in front of all these people that she was too good for him, that the community needed her more. She waited for Cy to tell her he was leaving tomorrow without her.

"Ellie, these last few days have been the first in months, no, in *years* that I let myself feel. When I saw what you'd done for my son at the pageant, when I realized what you've done for *me* since I got here, it all became clear. I can't lose you, and I can't take Jonty away from Rata Cove."

Her chest tightened and an icy blanket shrouded her body.

"Something you said to me when Jonty went missing from the hall suddenly made sense as I watched that pageant. For so long I've run when things got difficult. When my parents fought, when things became tough with Susan, when I didn't know what to do after William died. I did that after you'd found Jonty on the beach."

Ellie looked down. Every muscle in her body had slackened, and she held onto the lectern for support.

"I understand that deep down you still blame yourself for William's death, that you wonder if you could let yourself be responsible for a child again, but I've seen you do it. In these last two weeks, you've opened your heart to Jonty. You're confident and calm around him, and you make him believe he can do things. Not only do I love you for the way you do that for Jonty, I love you for the way you do it for me." His voice hitched. "The way you've challenged me in the last two weeks...you've healed me. Made me whole. I want us to do that for each other, day after day."

Ellie, when I close my eyes, I see your face. When I'm alone, I turn to look for you. When I imagine my life, my future, you're always in it. I love you. I can't live without you."

~

"No, you don't love me, Cy. You love the *idea* of me being with you and Jonty, to make things easier. But I don't want that life."

He shook his head. She was so damn rational. Didn't she *feel* it—what was between them? His chest clenched tight. "No. You're wrong."

"What you and I have is a deep and precious friendship, and that friendship will last a lifetime. You can still come back to Rata Cove as you did this time, just as the children and grandchildren of everyone here will. Every holiday. Every year. Nothing will change that."

A monster roared up in his mouth, ready to deny all she said, but he swallowed it. She had to see that everything was different now. That *he* was different. She'd made him this way. He loved her with his whole soul. He'd never been more certain of anything in his life. It might have taken a crazy Christmas week in a tiny little corner of the world, but day by day she'd swum into his heart and he wasn't going to let her leave it again. Ever.

"What you and I have is far more than friendship, Ellie."

Lines dug into the smooth skin of her forehead.

"What you and I have is love. Huge, undeniable love. God, I can't believe I've blinded myself to it."

"How do you know?" she said in a cracking whisper.

"When do you know the line between friendship and love has been crossed? Need? Want? Love? It's hard to tell which is which. I can't risk the life I've built for myself by trusting something so fragile."

"You won't have to."

She looked up at him and frowned. "What do you mean?"

"For some time now, my biggest competitor has been wanting to buy me out. Yesterday, I let him know I'm moving back to New Zealand, and we agreed on a price. I'd like to invest that money somewhere." He smiled at the wide-eyed look on her face. "Preferably in a coastal architecture firm that specializes in safeguarding people's memories. I want you to keep doing what you love so much, and I want to be by your side while you're doing it."

"I don't know what to say." Tears covered her lashes for a second before she blinked them away. "You'd do that for me? You'd help me build my business?"

"I've listened to you say you don't want children because you're too busy, too focused on other things. But I know the real reason is because you're scared of losing someone. What if you could do both? What if you could have your career and a family who love and support you? I want to help you do that, Ellie."

She blinked and hugged her arms tight against her body and he had to lock every muscle to stop himself from going to her.

"I love you, Ellie. I want you. I need you. They're all a part of me. I don't need to know the difference."

She drew a shaking hand across her forehead, and her eyes sparked. "Oh, Cy..."

He pulled her closer. "I don't want to live in the past anymore. I want to build a future with you. A future where you can do the work that's so important to you, with me by your side. A real future with a real family and real love." He pulled the ring box he'd collected from Auckland this morning from his pocket and dropped to his knee.

"I want to be your real husband. Will you marry me?"

Ellie's mind froze and everyone in the room held their breath as she looked down at the diamond solitaire they'd picked out together in Auckland.

He loved her. Wanted her. He believed she had what it took to be a real mother to his son. Her body buzzed as she tried to still her scattered thoughts. "What can I say, Cy?"

"Say yes and kiss him for God's sake," Betty Browning shouted from the back row, her camera lifted to her face.

Ellie laughed out loud and a wave of joy took off in her body.

"Say yes," Cy said as he looked into her eyes. "Just say that you feel the same and that you'll be my wife, for real this time."

"I love you, Cy. I've always loved you. Since you've been back, I've driven myself crazy trying to deny it, wanting to act like the friend I knew you needed. I buried it time after time. I can't do it anymore."

"I still need a friend." His voice hummed in her ear. "And you're the best there is."

She reached up and hooked a hand behind his neck and he kissed her long and slow as the hall erupted in whistles and shouts.

When she finally eased her lips from his, she grinned as he slipped the ring on her finger. "And don't we have a date at a registry office tomorrow, anyway?"

He shook his head. "Not anymore." A smile lit his face. "I want everything to be real from now on. And that includes the biggest, best wedding when you're ready. Not before. But there's one more thing."

"More?"

"Jonty's grandparents want to move back to New Zealand now and I've offered them my holiday house. That means you, me, and Jonty will need a new one..." His lips lifted in a teasing smile. "I was wondering if you knew any good architects."

Ellie pulled Cy to her again and pressed her lips to his. Creating a home for the man she loved and the little boy she couldn't imagine living without?

That was one project she couldn't wait to begin.

EPILOGUE

Jonty's grandma Maria leaned in and whispered, her breath warming Ellie's ear. "They're on next."

Ellie reached for the older woman's hand and Maria's deep brown eyes crinkled in a smile. "It's so lovely being here together." Ellie's voice quaked under the words. "It means everything to Jonty. And to us."

The older woman squeezed her hand. "Being here with you all is so special, Ellie. Especially getting to see our gorgeous grandson sing his lungs out with his cousin. This is really what the holiday season's all about, isn't it?"

Beside her, Cy leaned in. "Thanks, Maria. For the singing lessons. He's found a big voice in that little body."

Maria's face softened. They'd come a long way in a year, Susan's parents. Not only had Maria and Jeff moved back to New Zealand for good, at the beginning of December they'd moved into Cy's holiday home for the summer with Ellie, Cy, and Jonty. They were having a whale of a time.

"If it's another step in his recovery, that's all that matters," the older woman said.

Cy nodded. "Having you here has certainly helped him as well. He's so excited that you'll be seeing him onstage."

Maria's eyes glittered. "Susan would be so proud of what you've both done for him." She turned to her husband, who was trying to take a video on his phone.

The warm pressure of Cy's hand slipping into hers caused her heart to leap, as it always did. With his business in the States sold, Cy had opened surf schools throughout New Zealand. They lived in the cove most of the year, except for the times the three of them would visit Ellie's projects around the world.

"Here they come," Cy whispered. "Our boy and our nephew."

A moose took the stage—a little brown moose with cloth antlers that sagged over a small, round face lit like a city skyline. In a high and tuneful voice, he sang about life in the mountains—how he loved the sun on his hide and the grass under his hooves. Beside him, a woolly sheep in the shape of ten-year-old Louis joined in a chorus about being different, but just the same.

Ellie smoothed the blue-and-green silk scarf that lay across her knee. Jonty never wore it these days, but liked to keep it close by all the same. He'd left it in Ellie's care and her heart burst with pride for all the progress he'd made.

She turned around in her chair and smiled at her parents and Fleur, then at Cy's mum beside him. Nana Pat was back in the cove for the first time in years. Ellie and Cy were planning to build her a new house beside theirs. From deep within, a cocktail of tears and laughter fizzed through her. This place had always held such strong memories for them all.

Cy leaned in closer. "They're the United Nations of flora and fauna," he whispered. "Jonty's graduated from tree to beast, and Louis is just perfect as a sheep." Ellie turned her face to him and in the dim light, his eyes sparked.

They watched the rest of Jonty and Louis's performance and when it was finished, Ellie's hands ached from clapping, her mouth strained from smiling.

She snuggled closer to Cy, and he kissed her on the cheek. "I love you, Ellie Hathaway. I love what you've done for our boy, for his grandparents, and I love you for what you've done for me. I can't wait to move into our new house."

Ellie grinned. "It's looking so good. A brand-new house for a brand-new year."

"I don't know how we can beat the excitement of the last year," Cy said. "A marriage, a thriving business, and a place of our own." His smiling eyes sparkled, and she pulled him closer.

"We'll find a way." Familiar contentment soaked her. "We've got a whole life full of Christmas days, New Year's Eve pageants, and family get-togethers. They'll all be exciting, as long as I'm spending them with you."

The End

Thank you so much for reading *Desperate Measures*. I hope you love Cy and Ellie as much as I do!

If you'd like to find out what Kirin and Gwin are up to you can read **Bad Reputations~Kirin's story**, and **Missing Pieces~Gwin's story**. You can also receive a **FREE** prequel to my **Tall, Dark and Driven series**, *Waiting on Forever—Alex's story*, sign up to my newsletter **here**.

Find out what's happening for other characters of Brentwood Bay in the *Tall, Dark and Driven* series! You can find Book 1, *Making the Love List—Yasmin's story* **FREE** here, or ask for it at your local bookstore or library.

I hugely appreciate your help in spreading the word about my books, including telling a friend. Reviews help readers like you find my books! Please review *Desperate Measures* **here** or on your favorite site.

Turn the page for the blurb and an excerpt from Book 3 in the Breaking Through series, **Missing Pieces ~ Gwin's story.**

When the past walks back into your life, it can steal your heart.

Gwin Adams can't get out of Brentwood Bay quick enough. Apart from wanting to get her sister Ava and niece Rosie away from bad influences, she wants to finally break the chains of a tragic past. When that past in the form of a lost nephew and his adoptive father come knocking on her door, she has to choose between blowing everyone's world apart with the truth, or carrying on the secrets.

Single dad Mack Forde, is at the end of his tether. He's fiercely loved his sixteen year old son, Connor, since he and his ex wife adopted him as a baby, but Connor isn't just going off the rails, he's hurtling down the tracks so fast it's taking both their breaths away. Although he'd hoped reconnecting Connor with his biological family might help his beautiful son, he isn't prepared for his reaction to Gwin and her perfect, protecting heart.

As sparks fly between Gwin and Mack, they must tread a fine line between protecting everyone around them, and blowing their worlds apart.

Turn the page to read Chapter One of *Missing Pieces~ Gwin's story*

You can preorder *Missing Pieces~ Gwin's story here.*

MISSING PIECES - CHAPTER ONE

Guinevere Adams closed her eyes against the rain pummeling her windshield and the noise of the swishing wiper blades and tried to make another deal with God. Considering this was her fourth wager today with the big fella, and the fact he hadn't come up trumps on the last three could make anyone think they were low on his priority list. But then, she'd never been one to take a hint.

"Fifteen little minutes," she pleaded as she tapped her forehead against the steering wheel.

"Just stop long enough for me to take these boxes inside and then I'll do whatever you want." The low rumble of thunder in the distance mocked her pleading. "I'll be nice to everyone for twenty-four ..." She bit her lip and looked up at herself in the rear-view mirror. Who was she actually kidding?

"Twelve hours. I'll be good for twelve hours for Go—Murphy's sake."

The rain hammered harder and the branch of the tree she was parked next to whipped against her roof as if someone upstairs had kept tally of all the idiotic things she'd done this week and wasn't going to have a piece of this pathetic begging.

She let out a slow sigh and turned to look at the mountain of cardboard boxes on her back seat. The plan in her lunch hour had been to travel to the grocery store, pick up a pile of produce boxes for packing, hurry home and drop them in her room while her mom was at work before racing back to the office.

When she'd driven past their driveway ten minutes ago, a dirty great van was blocking it so now she was parked a whole block and a half away as great streams of muddy water pushed up against the trash and leaves clogging the town drains and ran down the center of the road. If she tried to make a run for it with these boxes, she'd end up at 3645 Westbrook with a pile of mush in her hands.

She flicked her wrist and frowned at her watch. Only twenty minutes before she had to be back at the office, and she <u>wasn't</u> going to leave these boxes until after work when her mom would purse her lips and doing that snuffling thing she did through her nose whenever there was any mention of moving.

Suddenly, she was aware of a shaft of light coming through her windshield. And where had the sound of the rain gone? She half expected a choir of archangels to start singing and Oprah to appear on her hood saying, "Guinevere Adams, on Tuesday this 6th day of June, we have decided that you deserve a big fat piece of luck."

Just as she was about to open the car door to make a run for it, her phone buzzed in her bag.

Breathing slowly through her nose, she reached in to grab it. It would either be her boss Nigel asking why she was taking so long and why she hadn't completed the order for

Trebullo's already or. . . She squinted at the screen. . . Her mom.

She swiped to talk.

"Are you okay?" her mother asked.

"Sure, why wouldn't I be? How's your day going? Did you make that doctor's appointment?"

"You're sitting in your car on Willow Avenue and it's pouring with rain," her mom said, ignoring her question.

Gwin's head whipped to the left and right, and then behind her. What the actual? Was Lonnie stalking her right now? Owning a hair salon meant her mom was the eyes and ears of Brentwood Bay and if she didn't know something, she'd find someone who did. Or make it up.

"Jilly Henderson saw you. She's come in for a cut and she was concerned 'cause you seemed to just be staring straight ahead. At nothing. And she wasn't sure if that was a real man in the passenger seat or one of your dummies."

Gwin could imagine the scene in her mom's beauty parlor. They'd all be discussing where Gwin might be going and what she might be doing when she got there, who she might be with, and boy what a shame it was that neither of the Adams girls had met a nice man and moved out of their mom's house, and if only Gwin could take a little care in the way she looked and the way her potty mouth ran away with her. . . Resentment prickled in her chest.

"I'm fine, Mom," she said as she started her engine, revving it a little for effect and ignoring the dummy comment. She looked across at torso-only-Troy, strapped into the passenger seat so he wouldn't break his plaster nose on the dash if she braked suddenly. He didn't even have man bits, for goodness sake—just a eunuch with a sneer on his face and a crack on his butt that needed fixing. "Thanks for checking," she said, neither confirming nor denying whether Troy was real. That'd leave the ladies guessing. "I've gotta get back to work."

"Okay," her mother said with that slow and drawn out way that suggested she didn't think things were okay at all. "You didn't stop by the house, did you?"

Her brain flipped an immediate 180. Should she lie and say she hadn't been near the place? Or would another one of her mother's clients have spotted her driving past there as well?

Her eye twitched. Anyone would think she was thirteen and had just climbed out the window to go to an all-night rave, or whatever the hell teenagers did these days, instead of a woman who was going to be thirty in November and doing everything she could to take charge of her life.

"I drove past," she said. "There's a big old truck outside."

"Oh, that's a guy working for Larry Brown. He asked me if they could park it there this morning. I wondered if Ava was home. I don't think she's been home all day. You'll be there for Rosie's birthday dinner tonight, right?"

When wasn't she home for dinner?

"Of course," she said as she pulled out into the traffic. "I ordered that red velvet birthday cake she loves. I'll pick it up on my way home. Now, will you make an appointment to get that mole checked."

"I told you, I've had that mole since I was twelve and it's got three hairs growing out of it. I looked it up on Check My Health and it said hairy moles are fine. I wouldn't put it past your sister to forget about Rosie's birthday. Her mother's tone mirrored Gwin's thoughts exactly. "Maybe you should call and remind her. She wasn't even up this morning before Rosie left for school."

Gwin wasn't even sure Ava had stayed at home last night. She'd been spending an awful lot of time with a new guy she'd been seeing, but none of them had met him yet. Her sister seemed to be completely enraptured with him and was always running when he summoned her.

"I don't like the sound of that new guy she's been seeing either," Lonnie continued. "I said to her what's the point in meeting someone and trying to have some kind of relationship just a month before you're moving <u>so</u> far away."

Nobody liked the sound of any of the guys her sister Ava went out with, but once these boxes were full of all their belongings, Gwin, Ava and Rosie would be out of here and all that would change.

There would be <u>good</u> guys in San Francisco, nice guys that didn't expect a bang in the back of their rusted-out Toyota Corolla before you even pulled out of the driveway on the way to your first date. Or guys who had actual interests rather than spending all day writing creepy messages on Tinder. Or maybe there would be <u>no</u> men. Maybe both she and Ava would find fabulous jobs that paid ridiculous salaries, Rosie would find a school that she loved, they'd find a great place to live and when Lonnie sold the beauty parlor, she could move down and they could all help create an exciting future for Rosie.

"Imagine if she stays because of him? Where would that leave you. . . with all your. . .plans?"

All your plans. Your cruel and selfish plans to move away and destroy my life after everything I've done for you.

With the deft skill of a contortionist, Lonnie had flipped the conversation back to why her, Ava, and Rosie moving away was a really bad idea. And Gwin knew from experience that this sort of conversation would only end with her feeling guilty and sad, and angry at herself for letting her mom get under her skin. "Sorry Mom, I can't hear you over the blow-dryers. Let's talk later."

"Can you stop by the grocery store on your way home?" Lonnie shouted into the phone. "I need five more of those minestrone labels to enter for that trip to Rome. It closes Saturday."

Gwin promised her mother the cans of soup, hung up and then moved out into the Brentwood Bay traffic that was struggling with this spring downpour. She pushed play on the car stereo and when the dramatic tones of Jessye Norman in the *Marriage of Figaro* filled her Nissan, she could feel her blood slow and her breathing equalize. The two times she'd seen this opera live it had been amazing, but nothing like the feeling of sitting by herself in her car, the volume turned right up and the hairs on the back of her neck rising with each new note.

Once, when she'd been listening to this same aria, she'd sat in the parking lot at work and just before the final notes were sung, Nigel had knocked on her window and she'd had to pretend she wasn't crying.

Stopping at the traffic lights beside Centennial Park she mouthed the Italian words, or at least the sounds of what she thought the words were. Maybe in the city she could find a night class that taught Italian, or maybe she'd get a season's ticket to the War Memorial Opera House and she could sit in the Gods and cry all she wanted.

A sizzle of excitement stirred her blood. In only six weeks she would say goodbye to this town that had squashed her to its bosom for the last twenty-nine years, and it couldn't come quick enough.

She drove on, passing Miss Tottie's pre-school where she and her sister Ava had spent long days while Lonnie worked to support them. Her mom had owned the Clip 'n Curl since their dad had left when she was a baby, something Gwin felt she remembered but was probably just born out of the dog-eared photos in the album her mom kept on the bookshelf by the fireplace. And the bitter stories Lonnie would recount of the marriage breakup whenever she'd had one too many Baileys on the rocks.

Ava's daughter Rosie had been to Miss Tottie's too, while Ava returned to high school for six months after she was born, until she got sick of the teasing and the knowing stares. Gwin would've stayed home to look after Rosie if she could've, but back then she was bringing in twice Lonnie's wage, and her hours meant she could be home with Rosie when Lonnie was doing her late nights and Ava was in night school.

She pulled into the parking lot of *Mannequin Mania*, cut the engine and let the final strains of Countess Rosina forgiving her husband trail to applause then got out and moved to the passenger door.

"Come on, Troy," she said as she clicked the seatbelt and pulled the mannequin from his seat. "Let's go get your butt crack fixed."

With Troy tucked under one arm, her bag on her shoulder, and her phone in the other hand, she clicked on speed dial for her sister and headed to the building. It took fifteen rings before Ava picked up.

"Hi, you sound sleepy," Gwin said when her sister answered. She stuffed her keys into her bag and rushed through the automatic doors. "Are you still in bed?"

"I might be," her sister said, a grin in her voice. "Not that there's been much *sleeping* going on."

One one thousand. Two one thousand. Jumping to quick judgement when it came to her older sister wasn't something Gwin was proud of, but sometimes there was no better option than to come straight to the point. "Oh my god, are you in bed with that guy? What's his name?" She took the stairs at double time. Damned if she was going to let her Fitbit mock her for the fifth night in a row.

Ava lowered her voice. "He's taking a shower, so I need to be quick. Is everything okay? Did you get the packing boxes?"

Gwin should remember the name of this guy, but to be brutally honest, she hadn't been fully listening when Ava had been describing him in detail yesterday. A list of all the guys Ava had dated in the past few years would fill the Brentwood Bay white pages a hundred times over. But it was understandable. After everything her precious sister had been through.

"Yes, I just picked them up. Does he know you're leaving town?" Gwin's breath shortened, and she cursed the custard jam donut she'd scarfed on the way to work this morning. There would be none of that in San Francisco. They'd shop organic and give up sugar, they'd do Barre or Zumba and there'd be no half-empty bottles of Southern Comfort in the pantry.

"No," her sister said, all cool and in control. "We haven't discussed tomorrow, let alone next month. He's pretty keen though."

"Are you seeing him tonight after Rosie's birthday dinner? Don't forget we're having takeout. And I'm getting a cake." She'd reached the top of the stairs and leaned against the cool, ornate column, panting like a bloodhound. "I think it'd be really good if we could just spend some more nights in with Mom, you know. Just the three of us. July's getting closer and I think we need to try and make things easy on her."

"Sure," her sister said before letting out a high-pitched shriek. Suddenly Ava's voice was muffled but Gwin heard something like, *My sister. I'm nearly done.*

"So, I'll see you tonight then?" Gwin said as she flashed a grin at Beth, the M and M receptionist. "Just you?"

"Gotta go," her sister said. The phone went dead.

"Beth!" a whispered voice hissed behind her. Beth was out of her seat behind the reception desk and beckoning her into the photocopy alcove. Today she wore purple pinstripe stovepipe pants tucked into shiny black Doctor Martin boots and a bottle green waistcoat. "Quick, before anyone sees you."

She hurried over and joined Beth behind the partition. "Mr. Trebullo's on the warpath," she whispered, sage green eyes searching hers. "He wants to know why his mannequins haven't been delivered yet. He said you promised they'd be ready at the start of this week, then Louise Hamilton rang and said that she's cancelling her contract because she heard you calling her dog a barking slipper."

Blood drained to her feet. Oh crap. She had said that about Louise Hamilton's dog to Nigel when they'd left Louise's office after the twelfth meeting in a row yesterday. And she wasn't sorry. That woman was as annoying as her dog. She had the same superior look in her eye, and she barked orders like a shitzu on meth.

As for Giovanni Trebullo, the only thing he cared about was making synthetic suits that he pretended were Italian wool. His mannequins were in a shocking state and anyone who treated them that badly deserved to wait. Troy was one of his, and Gwin had had to collect him from the dirty back office of one of Trebullo's stores. After the way he'd been treated, she wasn't completely sure she'd give him back.

"I told Trebullo you had period pain and went to the pharmacy for Advil," Beth said. "Doll, you look like complete shit. Are you okay?"

She swatted Beth. "Period pain! Thanks for reinforcing his misogynistic belief that every woman is incompetent."

"It stopped him asking, but," Beth said with a wink. "Where were you? You never take a lunch break."

"I had to pick up poor old Troy here. Look at the state of him, the poor love." She patted Troy's head. "Then I tried to get some packing boxes into the house without Mom seeing, and it was a complete failure."

"I don't know why you don't just hire Book-a-Beefcake for your move."

"Book a what?" Beth had worked at M and M for ten years and never failed to make Gwin feel better about life. God, she was going to miss her. And Nigel. The three of them had had so much fun in the last few years building the business Nigel had inherited from his father. They'd grown from a tiny plant that manufactured fashion store mannequins to a thriving design, repair and redevelopment studio that made everything from mannequin babies to zombies. That tiny little twang of terror and thrill and sadness that she was leaving this life behind sparked for a second before she squashed it flat.

"Book-a-Beefcake are literally these two built dudes who wear those itty-bitty gym tops and they can lift a grand piano with their little finger. They just pull up in their semi, swoop in and pack everything up, and then they're out of there in no time. Lonnie wouldn't have a chance to complain."

Gwin chewed her lip. "It's costing so much as it is with putting aside the rental bond and the fact that Ava doesn't have a job yet, and all the things we're going to have to pay for Rosie's new school."

"I can loan you the money, hun. You're going to be back on your feet in no time and you can pay me back then."

Love for her friend swelled inside her. "It's okay," she said, touching Beth's arm. "Mom's getting used to it. I really need to stop trying to protect her. She's actually seemed a lot better about it lately. And besides, you're not lending any money to anyone. You're enrolling in your screen writing course. You promised. If you don't do it soon, I'm going to do it for you."

"Beth?" Nigel's voice was a forced whisper through the intercom. "Is Gwin back yet? Trebullo's on his way to find her and he's not happy."

"I'm here, Nige," she whispered back loudly. "I'm going to tell him they're more damaged than we thought and it's going to take an extra week, okay? They're in an appalling state." Poor Nigel, he hated dealing with clients and should be back in the studio doing the creative stuff that he loved, but his father "Big Nigel" had retired at the end of last year and Nigel was doing his best to lead the company.

She moved out of the cubicle, and Beth put her hand on Gwin's shoulder. "Lonnie will be fine. She's lived in Brentwood Bay her entire life and she's got a bajillion friends. She'd hate it in the city. You know that deep down, and its time you put yourself first instead of worrying about Ava and your Mom."

"You're right," she said on a long sigh. "When we first talked about it, we completely expected that she'd come with us, but she just refuses. And it's the right time to move with Rosie about to start high school, but it's always been the four of us. It's kinda petrifying you know?"

Beth's eyes twinkled. "You're gonna smash it, babe. You should've done it years ago."

"Nigel, if you can't find her then I'm going to take my business elsewhere." Mr. Trebullo's voice carried the length of the corridor. The way he treated those mannequins, Gwin wouldn't mind betting he treated his family poorly as well.

They both looked around the cubicle as her client came marching toward her, his face like a baboon's booty. Gwin willed it July already, their goodbyes done, dodgy boyfriends given the slip, and a sparkling new life just theirs for the taking.

You can preorder *Missing Pieces~ Gwin's story here.*

FANCY A FREE NOVELLA?

Throughout my career, my readers have been such a key part of my writing life, and I love to keep them up to date with what I'm doing. I occasionally send out newsletters with details on new releases and extra special offers for both my books and others like mine. I promise I won't bombard you!

If you sign up to the mailing list, the first thing I'll send you is a **FREE** novella, ***Waiting on Forever***, is Alex and Mara's story, and the prequel to my ***Tall, Dark and Driven*** series.

Waiting on Forever

One last task to complete, then Alex Panos can fulfill a heart-breaking promise. That is, if he can get past cute and quirky Mara Hemmingway.

On her own since she was sixteen, Mara won't be taken advantage of again—especially not by brooding and troubled Alex. Instead, she'll play him at his own game.

When their powerful attraction threatens to get in the way of

APPLY TO JOIN BARBARA'S REVIEW TEAM!

If you really enjoyed *Desperate Measures* and fancy reading a lot more about the crazy, lovable people of Brentwood Bay and beyond, apply to join Barbara's review team!

Barbara is now taking applications to join her Advanced Review team. If you're selected, you'll get all of Barbara's releases free, up to a month before release!

Fill out an application **here** or email: barb@barbaradeleo.com

ALSO BY BARBARA DELEO

The Breaking Through series

All books can be read as stand alone.

Bad Reputations—Book 1 ~Kirin's story ~ available on Amazon here or ask for it at your local bookstore or library.

———————————

The Tall, Dark and Driven series

All books can be read as stand alone

Waiting on Forever—prequel novella ~ **Alex's story** ~ available **FREE** here or email barb@barbaradeleo.com

Making the Love List —Book 1 ~ **Yasmin's story** available FREE here or ask for it at your local book store or library.

Winning the Wedding War —Book 2 ~ **Nick's story** available here or ask for it at your local book store or library.

Reining in the Rebel—Book 3 ~ **Ari's story** available here or ask for it at your local book store or library.

A Home for Summer —Book 4 ~ **Costa's story** available here or ask for it at your local book store or library.

A Marriage for Show —Book 5 ~ **Christo's story** available here or ask for it at your local book store or library.

A Family for Good—Book 6 ~ Markus's story available here or ask for it at your local book store or library.

ABOUT BARBARA

Multi award winning author, Barbara DeLeo's first book, co-written with her best friend, was a story about beauty queens in space. She was eleven, and the sole, handwritten copy was lost years ago much to everyone's relief. It's some small miracle that she kept the faith and now lives her dream of writing sparkling contemporary romance with unforgettable characters.

Degrees in English and Psychology, and a career as an English teacher, fueled Barbara's passion for people and stories, and a number of years living in Europe —primarily in Athens, Greece—gave her a love for romantic settings.

Discovering she was having her second set of twins in two years, Barbara knew she must be paying penance for being disorganized in a previous life and now uses every spare second to create her stories.With every word she writes, Barbara is sharing her belief in the transformational power of loving relationships.

Married to her winemaker hero for twenty two years, Barbara's happiest when she's getting to know her latest cast of characters. She still loves telling stories about finding love in all the wrong places, but now without a beauty queen or spaceship in sight.

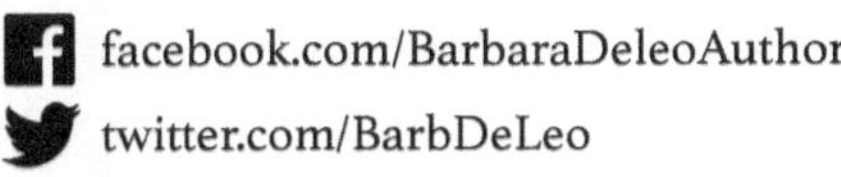

Desperate Measures
Ellie's story
A *Breaking Through* book
by Barbara DeLeo

Cover Design - Natasha Snow Designs www.natashasnow.com